The Genuine Article

The Genuine Article

a novel by

A. B. GUTHRIE, JR.

BOSTON
HOUGHTON MIFFLIN COMPANY
1977

c.1

W

Library of Congress Cataloging in Publication Data

Guthrie, Alfred Bertram, date
  The genuine article.

  I. Title.
PZ3.G95876Ge [PS3513.U855] 813'.5'2 77-2248
ISBN 0-395-25361-6

Printed in the United States of America

S 10 9 8 7 6 5 4 3 2 1

BL

To Alice and Kenneth
friends through the years

If anyone wants to find a resemblance
between himself and any of my characters,
let him.

The Genuine Article

Chapter One

F. Y. GRIMSLEY hated Indians, full-blood, half-blood, quarter-blood and any with a known fraction of taint. That much I knew as I listened to him bitching to Sheriff Chick Charleston, that much and more.

Grimsley had a sizable cattle ranch in the southwest corner of the county. What with owned and leased land, it amounted to twenty thousand acres, give or take a stray section or two.

"It's your job, Charleston. Get up in the collar!" Grimsley was saying for the fifth or sixth time if not in the same words. He took his hat off and slapped it on his knee, losing about an acre of dust from the ranch. His head, scarred high on the dome, was so bald that, seen along with the scar, you could have sworn he had had a skin graft.

F. Y. Grimsley, standing for Frank Yantis Grimsley, as I already knew, thanks to a plat of the county. A lot of people didn't like him for one reason or another, all good, and used his initials for words appropriate to their feelings.

"Five hundred cows, plus calves, some here, some there," Charleston said. His head moved in a slow shake. "We'll scout around, but we can't keep steady watch on all that beef." As nearly always, his tone was mild.

"Did I ask you for that? No, by God! Just find out. Be a detective for once, like you're paid for. Have a look, listen and add two and two if you're up to it."

Charleston shied a glance at me. "Jase, here, knows his figures. Just back from college."

Grimsley snorted. "You ain't funny, and it ain't college brains I'm in need of. Them professors don't know ass from sassafras. So cut out the cracks! Get into action!"

"Any particular place?"

"On my ranch. Where the hell else?"

"That's not so particular."

"Goddamn! You think I can scout every gulley night and day? What I know is I'm losing stock."

"Singles or bunches?"

"Singles, maybe. Two or three at a time, maybe. Who knows? Here's one case. I had some in my west field. Forty cows, thirty-four calves. Yesterday the tally showed thirty-seven cows and thirty-one calves. No dead ones around. None coyote-killed. There you are. Your move, Mr. Sheriff." Grimsley's mouth was as small and as round and as tight as a bullet hole.

"Any signs of butchering?"

"No. No guts at all."

"You mentioned Breedtown."

"Sure. It's somebody there; more'n one, likely. I'll bet my butt on that. They ought to wipe that place off the map. Bunch of squatters. No rights."

"That land under lease?"

"No. Government-owned. I'd lease it myself except it doesn't amount to shit, bar Eagle Charlie's eighty acres."

"He owns that?"

"Where in Christ's name does that figure? Yes. He got title to it, don't ask me how. Only piece of land around there worth a damn. Has that nice spring on it."

"What about Eagle Charlie?"

"For an Indian he ain't so bad. I said, for an Indian. It's them hangers-on, aunts and uncles and cousins and nephews and all them inbreds and God knows what."

Eagle Charlie, I thought. Short for Sees Eagle Charbonneau, my father had told me. A cross between Indian and French and no known relation to the Charbonneau who got famous by being married to Sacajawea in the days of Lewis and Clark.

"You've talked to Eagle Charlie?" Charleston asked.

"All this fool palaver!" Grimsley answered. It looked as if he might wham his hat again and lose another acre of ground. "It don't do no good to talk to Charlie. Them ragged-tailed Indians don't pay any attention to him, even if some call him chief."

"No chiefs ever had much authority. No downright say-so."

"I'll remember that when I ain't thinkin' about something important."

"Tell me more about Charlie. How does he get by?"

"Charleston, you're askin' for what you already know. Just killin' the by-God time. All right. That spring of Charlie's waters a garden. Potatoes and rutabagas and such. His poor goddamn wife does all the work. I know that."

"He wouldn't charge the others for water from his spring." Charleston shook his head. "No Indian would."

"Naw, not as I know of. He works once in a while, gettin' logs out and helpin' come hay-time. Kills a deer when he needs it, in season or out. He does all right, what with his garden and a couple of milk cows."

"Those relatives squat on his land?"

"Not so much. Just visitors once in a while. The rest camp out around. You know, shacks, log cabins and maybe a tent or two, depending. They ought to be on the reservation, the whole kit and caboodle."

"No place set aside for them. They're landless Indians, Chippewas and Crees mostly."

"They don't belong where they are. Neighbors to my cows, thievin' neighbors."

"The Indians had the land in the first place."

Now for the second time Grimsley did slap his hat on his knee. One hand swiped at a cloud of dust. "You think I come here to fight the Indian wars all over again! I'm just askin' help, some simple goddamn help."

Charleston sighed and said, "All right, Grimsley. We'll do what we can."

"You better. Right away?"

"Right away."

"One thing I damn near forgot," Grimsley said while he made a pointer of his beat-up hat. "You know that walkin' ladder that swamps out saloons?"

"Luke McGluke."

"That's his name. And you know his automobile that no poor-ass junk dealer would give room in his yard to? Well, a couple or three times I've passed him on the road, bound Breedtown-way. Think on that."

"Thanks. I'll remember."

"I want results," Grimsley said. He got up, put his hat on his skin graft and went out.

Charleston smiled at me, not with any great mirth. "Joyful job, public office is."

I said, "I guess he can stand to lose a beef or two."

"Not the question, Jase. The law's the law—but pisswillie."

So things stood that late afternoon. The next morning F. Y. Grimsley was dead.

Chapter Two

I LAZED UP the street after leaving the sheriff's office, renewing acquaintance with 'those I hadn't renewed it with in the two days since my return. The June sun was sinking. It hadn't shed much warmth even at its height. June is a chancy month in my country.

After two years away—a long time in my reckoning then—I had expected a lot of changes in Midbury, but I hadn't noticed many. Same old place. Same people around, except that Otto Dacey, the one man in the county certified sane, wasn't wetting his pants or the gutter anymore, the Lord having taken him away. In his place as saloon swamper was this Luke McGluke, who was as sane as Otto and just as worthy of notice. He stood about six feet seven when he straightened his hinges and was as spooky as any wild goose.

I had seen him just yesterday and learned something about him. His real name, which nobody seemed to know, wasn't Luke McGluke. We had a habit in our town of giving men handles from old cartoon characters or made up from whim or actual initials. Some of them had a bite to them.

Felix Underwood stood in the last sun outside his parlors. He called himself a mortician now, perhaps because undertaker was too close to the quick. I shook hands with him.

"Hear you're hooked up with Chick Charleston again," he said.

"Yep. Back to being sheriff's flunky." I didn't tell him that I was a sure-enough deputy, though he might have heard so already. That news would get around soon enough.

The fact was that I could hardly believe it myself. Yesterday, when I had called on Charleston, he had offered me a badge. "Wait," I told him. "You know I'm not quite of age."

"You're registered for the draft, aren't you?"

"Yes. For some time."

"Well?" He raised one eyebrow.

I didn't have any answer.

"No one's going to squawk," he went on, "and I'm short of men. The town and county made a deal a month or two ago, and as a result this office will play town marshal. I have Halvor Amussen ticketed for that job. He'll need help, some from you. He's on vacation now. Back soon."

"Halvor?" I said. "Town marshal? To see girls don't get raped?"

Charleston gave me his good smile. "Halvor's in love and safe enough now. That girl he's stuck on will kill him if he tries to play rooster."

"I see old Jimmy Conner is still around."

"Right. Still my inside man, mostly. And Monk Fitzroy will stay up north at Petroleum. Even with you deputized, I'm still shy on staff. If someone likely comes to your mind, let me know. Here's your badge."

Now Felix Underwood said to me, "Was I you, I'd wonder about going back to the sheriff's office. Look at last time."

"My hand healed up well enough."

"Oh, did it now?" he said, his head shaking a no. Felix was a baseball fan and managed the town team when he could recruit enough players. "Not good enough to give a hop or a curve to a ball?"

"No, but good enough to write or serve papers or even, come to that, hold a gun."

"A good pitcher ruint," he told me.

My pitching days had ended when a crazy psychiatrist had batted my hand with a six-gun two years ago. Not that I cared much anymore. One year to go, and I'd be out of college and ready, as they say, for the real world. Mad psychiatrists weren't counted as real.

"You watch out, Jase," Felix said. "Burnt once should be enough."

The Jackson Hotel, the Commercial Cafe and the Bar Star Saloon stood as before, all showing signs of life as the working day ended. I went into the saloon for a beer. Though the law at that time said you had to be twenty-one if you had anything alcoholic, the management figured that the use of a razor qualified you for a drink. The bar was old-fashioned. It had three tables, one rounded for card players, and a fairly long counter complete with brass footrest and spittoons. A jukebox stood in one corner but wasn't used much. The common-run customer was a rancher or ranch hand or other outdoor worker who didn't mix hard liquor with hard rock.

Old Doc Yak was there, spindly as ever, chasing a homeopathic pill with a jigger of whiskey. F. Y. Grimsley was inside, too, talking to Junior Hogue and whoever would listen. He had had time for a couple of drinks before my arrival. Tad Frazier had moved up in life, from handyman to bartender. He was drawing a beer for Hogue.

These men I knew. I didn't know a young, well-built one who had red hair that reached from his turned-brim Stetson to the collar of his leather jacket. His attention was on the Coke that he sipped. Neither did I know two others. They stood off by themselves, maybe because they had a copper cast to their skins and knew Grimsley's feelings.

Refreshed by his formula of pill and Old Pebbleford, Doc Yak said, "Welcome home, Jason." He gave me his hand. Hogue interrupted Grimsley's talk long enough to say, "Hi." I had shaken hands with him yesterday.

"What portent in your return, Jason?" Doc Yak asked, adding with a smile as the events of two years ago came to his mind, "Trouble again?"

"I'm not contagious."

"No. Only diseases are."

Hogue had overheard our conversation, even while listening to Grimsley. He called out, "Tad, shake a leg. See what Typhoid Mary will have."

Tad did and then pumped my hand with his wet one.

"I'll tell you again, Hogue," Grimsley was saying, the whiskey talking loud in him, "and I'll warn everybody." His eyes traveled the bar and came to rest on the two breeds, a name we used for anyone with a touch of Indian blood in him. "I'll shoot any trespassers on sight, right away, pronto, night or day."

Though they must have heard him and felt his hard stare, the breeds showed no outward notice.

Hogue asked, "Why warn me? I got cows of my own."

"I'm warnin' the world."

"Law or no law?"

"The goddamn, son-of-a-bitchin' law! Pussycats. Fraidy-cats."

The redhead lifted his Coke. I thought I saw a look of distaste on his face. The breeds worked at their beers. It is surprising how long a man can make a beer last if he hasn't cash enough for another.

Hogue wasn't one to pass over a slur on a friend. His thumb jerked toward me as he spoke to Grimsley. "By any chance are you referrin' to Jase here?"

"Just a general idea," Grimsley replied, maybe a little as if in apology.

He was saved from any real ruction by the entrance of Luke McGluke, who shied away from the bar on his way to the rear.

"Boo!" Grimsley yelled at him.

McGluke didn't increase his pace, since he was already traveling at about three strides to the mile. As he let himself out, into the lean-to in the rear, he threw a look over his shoulder. I saw a frightened hate in his face.

"Spooks easy, that half-wit bastard," Grimsley said, the words trailing after him as he made for the door.

When he had gone, Hogue said, "That character has lived too long."

"Blame it on me," Doc Yak put in. "I doctored him for pneumonia last winter."

"That makes you pardner to the crime of him living," Hogue said. "What do you call it, Jase?"

The redhead answered. "Aiding and abetting, with equal responsibility."

I said, "That's close enough."

"For my sins I'll buy another round," Doc Yak said.

Tad filled the orders, omitting the breeds according to custom. The redhead asked for another Coke. I introduced myself to him.

Hogue interrupted us. "I'm awful forgetful of manners."

"They call me Red Fall." The man had a good grip.

"He drinks slop and wrangles dudes for Guy Jamison," Hogue told me.

"Just say I drink slop," Fall said, apparently not offended. "No dudes to wrangle for two or three weeks yet."

"Strayed from the south somewheres," Hogue went on.

"Southwest." Again Fall spoke, unruffled.

Doc Yak said, "Drink up. Time's wasting." I never had known him to waste so much time or to have more than one drink.

After he had drained his glass, he turned to me. "Don't turn up any more dead bodies, boy."

The remark struck me as thoughtless and out of order. Hogue's father had been shot dead two years before. But there was Doc Yak for you.

Chapter
Three

"TOO EARLY for red raspberries," my mother told me. I knew she had scouted the town for my favorite fruit. "I did find some strawberries, though."

I smiled at her and said my thanks.

We were seated—Dad, Mother and I—at the family table, eating home cooking, which was treat enough for me.

Dad was preoccupied, not gruff or unpleasant, just preoccupied, and I knew he would speak his thoughts soon, as he did.

"I suppose you saw that revival tent going up across the creek, Jase?" He was shaking his head.

"Just a glimpse of it."

His head kept moving. "I had thought we were beyond and away from such foolishness."

I said, "Oh?"

"I mean primitive religion," he went on. "Redneck stuff as preached in the south. Hysterical nonsense. I suppose this evangelist—Brother Sam he calls himself, short for Brother Samuel Muir—I suppose he wore out his welcome in Oklahoma." A half-smile came to Dad's mouth. "Or for the moment saved everyone there."

"Now don't be extreme, Father," Mother said.

"You haven't been exposed as I have," Dad told her. "I can still hear the holy whine of those soul-savers. I have seen the converted knuckleheads hitting the sawdust trail, as they say. I have seen people with the jerks and heard the babble of unknown tongues. Obscene, I say."

To keep him going, I said, "But you're religious, Dad."

"To an extent. To an extent." He paused to gather his thoughts. "I go to church, believing that, despite fable and superstition, it is a force for good. Religious? Religious in the sense that I believe in Christian principles of conduct. I take no stock in the ignorance that thinks it has heard God's call to save sinners. Primitives! Holy rollers! Healers! Foot washers! Snake handlers! The devil with them!"

Dad realized of a sudden that he had worked up quite a head of steam. A smile came to his face. "You've been leading me on, Jase."

After the dishes were done, after living-room talk not related to religion, we went to bed.

At 6 A.M., before her own getting-up time, Mother woke me up to say I was wanted on the telephone. Dawn had given way to a gray day. Charleston was on the line. He asked me to come to the office as soon as I could.

Jimmy Conner, who usually had something to say, gave me only a nod as I passed into the inner office. That was his way of indicating serious business. Charleston sat inside, talking to a little hard knot of a man whom he introduced as Dave Becker.

"Becker found F. Y. Grimsley dead at his doorstep early this morning," Charleston said. "We're going out there."

"Had a regular goddamn furrow in his head," Becker explained to me. "Not a furrow, though. No skin turned

over. A trench-like, it was." As Charleston got up, so did
he. I saw then that his legs must have been shaped by a
horse, a fat one.

"Jase, take time to call Doc Yak and Felix Underwood.
Then we'll go. I'll bring you back to town, Becker."

Neither Doc nor Felix seemed delighted at being called
so early, though Felix perked up when I said the dead
man was Grimsley. Grimsley's estate could afford funeral
expenses. Doc Yak wouldn't have been pleased in any
case. He said over the phone, "Damn your young soul, you
said you weren't contagious."

We filed out to the car. I had a pad and a couple of
pencils. I knew something about shorthand, though I seldom used it, relying on my memory instead.

The car was Charleston's old Special, which could run
like a jackrabbit and had even more clearance. It was
quiet enough that, from the back seat, I could hear what
Charleston and Becker said.

"And you told me you were first up?" Charleston asked.

"Yep. Always am. Been with Grimsley ten years. I was
comin' from the bunkhouse when I saw him lyin' there."

"Already dead?"

"Dead as a slab of lutefisk. Cold as a fish, too."

"And you got right in the pickup?"

"Sure. Didn't need to be told what to do, not with the
boss dead. So here I am, and out of a job to boot."

"What was Grimsley doing?"

"Nothin'. I said he was dead."

"Sorry. Before then, I mean. Why outside?"

"How do I know? Goin' or comin' from the privy, I
guess."

"No indoor plumbing? A man like Grimsley?"

"None of that. He always said a flush toilet constipated him."

The country roads had improved in the two years I had been away. The county had bought a rock crusher, which had pulverized some boulders and given a beating to others that a scraper had tumbled off to the side. A light rain was falling, and the landscape was misted so much that the mountains to the west were just hazy lines. We made good time.

Grimsley's place had a verandahed house at the front and a helter-skelter of outbuildings in the rear. A calf, an orphan I supposed, was blatting out there.

"Who else is here?" Charleston asked as Becker led the way to the back.

"Nobody," Becker answered. "Damn cook up and left last week, and Grimsley was scouting around for more help. We been bachin'. A little more of his grub and I'd be lyin' dead with him. There, now. See for yourself."

Grimsley lay, face up, near the back doorstep. He had his clothes on, the same clothes I had seen in town. His bullet mouth was open, but what struck you, first off, was the indentation in his bare skull. At the moment one glimpse was enough for me. The depression appeared long, blood-spotted and at its edges swollen and red.

Charleston knelt by the body. "You haven't moved him?" he asked Becker.

"Not by an inch, except I felt his wrist. No pulse, and his hand was as cold as hung beef."

Charleston lifted the head, which moved stiff. The mark made by whatever had killed Grimsley ran from front to back, over the curves. Charleston put out his hand to pick at the wound. What I saw chilled me then—four red hairs, medium long. It was as if the skin-graft head had sprouted growth overnight. Charleston put the hairs in an envelope, saying nothing.

Doc Yak drove up, scratching gravel. He was out of his car before it came to a stop. The car quit rolling when it bumped the corner of a shed, which put a small dent in one fender. Felix Underwood followed him, driving an ambulance.

Doc Yak bustled up to us, his satchel in his hand. He didn't take time for a greeting. He bent down and looked at the wound. His hand explored it and felt the flesh of wrist and chest.

Charleston waited until Doc straightened up. Then he asked, "How long would you say?"

"How in hell do I know?"

"Dead for some time, I would say." It was Underwood speaking. He had moved up beside Doc.

Charleston said, "That's kind of indefinite. Come off it now, Doc. Give me an estimate."

"Six, seven, eight hours. I'll know better later."

"Couldn't be more than seven," Becker put in. "I found him about sunup."

"And never even put a towel over his face?" Underwood said, respecting the dead. "You could have done that."

"Sure. I could have planted him, too, and saved you the trouble."

Charleston was casting around, maybe looking for footprints, looking for anything that might be a clue. He turned toward me and shook his head.

Underwood asked him, "Well?"

"Might as well. The body doesn't tell me anything more."

"Just the old blunt-instrument job, huh?"

Charleston's hand ran the shape of a skull in the air. "When did blunt instruments get flexible?"

"Should have seen that. Make it a blackjack."

I helped Underwood place the body on a stretcher and carry it and roll the stretcher into the back of the ambulance. Already Doc Yak was reversing his car, though he bumped the shed again first, having chosen the wrong gear.

Charleston wanted to inspect the house. Becker led the tour. We found nothing inside but the disorder expected of a man living alone.

We were silent on the return, silent until we were again in the sheriff's office where, after Jimmy Conner had reported a quiet morning, we sat down.

"A few more questions, Becker," Charleston said. "I gather you didn't hear anyone prowling around last night?"

"That's what I told you, and that's the truth, the whole truth and nothing but the by-God truth."

"Or see anyone, not a shadow of anyone?"

"True again."

"No noises? Nothing?"

"I heard a cow bawl. Or was it a calf?"

"No need to smart off, Becker."

"No need to ask questions I've answered already."

"All right. What about enemies? Did Grimsley have bad trouble with anyone lately?"

"No more'n usual."

"What do you mean by that?"

"All ranchers got troubles, one way or another."

"Yesterday he told me someone was making off with his beef."

"Did he, now?"

"He pointed toward Breedtown."

"He had a down on Indians in general."

"And he was losing cows?"

"One now and then. Maybe two."

"Did you yourself suspect anyone, you yourself?"

"Nope."

"What about Eagle Charlie?"

"Him and Grimsley got along fair enough."

"You said you'd been working for Grimsley for ten years. Did you know him before?"

"Never laid eyes on him. I was a long piece away, workin' in west Texas and then around the Tonto Basin."

"Mogollon Rim country."

"Right. Different from here, but cows is cows."

"What is your opinion of Grimsley? Did you like him, dislike him, hate him?"

"He paid pretty good, and he paid prompt."

"That's all you have to say?"

"What else? Never speak bad of the dead. That's what my old man taught me."

"This is a murder case, Becker. Don't you want to find out who killed your boss?"

"That's your job."

Charleston sighed and rose from his chair. "You'll stick around?"

"Till somep'n shows up."

"Do that. I advise you to do that."

Becker walked to the door. I thought again he needed a horse under him.

Charleston sat down as the door closed. "I guess you'd better take a tour around town, Jase. Better show we're playing town marshal."

"All right, but there's some things—" I began, thinking to tell him about being at the Bar Star and what happened there.

"Not now. They can wait."

I was letting myself out when he said, "Jase, Becker knows more than he tells. We'll have to work on him."

Chapter
Four

I ARRIVED early next morning before Charleston himself had appeared. Jimmy Conner was at his outside desk, though. You could count on him for everything except physical exercise. The office being shy on staff, he had installed a cot at one side of the room. He slept there, he told me, while Amussen was on vacation.

Chatting with him, I thought it didn't matter much to him where he bedded down. His wife was a practical nurse and often away from home, a fact that seemed to make for good marital relations.

"All you need," I said, "is a cookstove and a cupboard of groceries. Then you'd never have to move out."

"Kid," he answered, "when you've quit drinking and lost your taste for women, what do you do? Gamble? Hell, I can't afford it except for penny ante, and where's the fun in a two-bit pot? What is left to a man is work, plain damn work."

I told him, "You could live on memories, Jimmy. Days of old."

He shook his head. "That's pretty poor fodder, even if I was a kind of heller once."

As I was about to walk on, he said, "You won't see much of the sheriff this morning. Two sales scheduled."

"I have a report to type up, anyhow," I said.

His thumb jerked toward the jail in back. "Maybe you can find time to bring back some grub. I got a customer."

He saw the question in my eyes and went on, "You wouldn't know him. Some joker by the name of Curt Smith. I had to bring him in myself, after that new Safeway manager had cornered him with a leg of lamb under his coat."

"If he was that hungry," I said, "he'll want something to eat. I'll fetch it at noon, Jimmy."

Conner thanked me as I made for the inner office. He had feet that didn't like to take him even the two short blocks to the Commercial Cafe.

I went to a typewriter, carrying the brief notes I had taken, and inserted a blank page. I had a good memory. Once Charleston had said it was phenomenal. I began typing.

I had tapped out a page when Charleston came in, looking like the sheriff he was—frontier pants, jacket to match, white shirt with a tie, stockman's hat. He said, "Money before murder, Jase. It's sheriff-sale day. See you this afternoon."

I told him I'd have the report on yesterday ready.

He nodded and said, "Good. And if you find time, play town marshal maybe once before I get back. The taxpayers like to see their money at work, even when it buys nothing."

He went out.

I was all through at ten-thirty and left the office and got in the official town car, which was labeled CITY POLICE. This morning a marshal was about as much use as a stray dog. Mike Day lounged in front of his bank, his two En-

glish setters asleep on the sidewalk beside him. Mabel
Main, who hung on as telephone operator when all but
she had fled, came striding down the street, walking high-
kneed. A half-block behind her came Luke McGluke, who
kept looking behind him. He wasn't in a hurry. He
couldn't help going fast, being so high in the thigh. I
wondered what a cross between them would look like.
Probably a skyhook.

The road across the creek brought me in close sight of
the revival tent. It was all pitched apparently. A couple of
men were unloading folding chairs from a truck and carrying them in. The tent canvas was gray and a little tattered but covered a space big enough for a one-ring cir-
cus. A tall, gaunt man came out of an opening, looked at
the sky and nodded his head as if in thanks for fair
weather.

The day had turned bright and hot for June. What rain
had fallen yesterday had been sucked up, and dust rose
behind my wheels even though they rolled slow.

Just a little before noon I parked by the Commercial
Cafe and went in for a sandwich and the plate I had
promised to take back to the jail. Bodie Dunn was already
eating, and so was Frank Featherston. Neither were close
friends of mine, so I just waved and said, "Hi." Jessie Lou
was still slinging hash. I shook hands with her before I took
a seat at the counter. She had grown into quite a girl, from
bone and stringy muscle into full bloom.

After she had brought my order, I asked, "Do you work
night and day, Jessie Lou?"

"Not always," she answered, smiling. "Tonight I'm off
at ten-thirty." Her words seemed to carry a suggestion, a
half-invitation. She followed them with "Will you be in
again tonight?"

"Maybe for a bite later on," I told her, and she nodded as if pleased.

A couple of customers entered and took stools, and she went to wait on them.

At the office I gave the covered plate and cup of coffee to Jimmy Conner. He liked to wait on his guests himself, maybe because he was past getting into trouble on his own hook and liked to talk to those who could do it.

Charleston came into the inner office right after I did. I handed him my typed report.

"It can wait," he said, laying it aside. "You had something of your own you wanted to tell me?"

So I told him about being at the Bar Star, about Grimsley and Doc Yak and Red Fall and Junior Hogue and the two breeds I didn't know.

I said, "Yesterday, though, I got their names from Ted Frazier, after I left you."

He smiled. "Good for you, boy."

"One is Pete Pambrun," I reported, "and the other Framboise. No first name."

Charleston took a slow breath, and his eyes studied the ceiling. "Good old names. A Pambrun was a respected factor in the old fur-trade days, and Framboise or LaFramboise—means raspberry in English—one hell of an expedition leader on the route from Oregon to California. Ask your dad."

Sometimes it seemed to me that Charleston knew everything—everything now but who killed Grimsley.

I asked, "Have I told you anything important? Grimsley, kind of pretending not to, was giving those two breeds what-for."

Charleston's gaze came back from the ceiling. "Who knows, Jase? I'm sort of interested in that Luke McGluke.

Don't ask me why. Maybe Red Fall, too. When Amussen comes back, I may want you to keep an eye on McGluke. Dave Becker's my immediate meat. Now why don't you take the rest of the afternoon off? I want you on duty tonight."

"Duty?" I said.

Charleston gave me that good smile of his. "Town marshal again. Attend the revival meeting and save your soul."

When I didn't answer, he explained, "Wherever people gather, there can be trouble. That's the reason for special policemen at big events. Not that this event is so big that I expect trouble, but you better be there in case."

It doesn't take much to draw a crowd in a small town. Anything a little out of the ordinary will attract people whose lives are ordinary. That's what I thought as I parked the police car across the creek from the tent and saw through the trees that a congregation was gathering. The members were moving to the tent in fours and twos and singles, and the sounds of the voices I was able to hear didn't seem like the sounds of true worshipers. The people were coming in cars across the big bridge and parking where they could and then stringing along toward the tent. No one came my way while I sat there.

After watching and listening, I got out of the car, walked the path through the bushes, crossed the footbridge and went into the back of the tent, all along trying to be inconspicuous. The time was eight o'clock, and the long summer sunlight was heating the canvas as well as the crowd. I waited.

A stage, draped in white, had been set at the front of the

tent. An altar, I supposed it was called, stood on it. Beside and a little behind it were two chairs and a piano and stool. I couldn't see a loudspeaker. It turned out none was necessary.

After the last of the audience had dribbled in, making up a crowd of maybe a hundred and twenty-five people, the evangelist came in through a side door and mounted to the pulpit. After him came a pianist, who seated herself on the piano stool, a snare drummer with a couple of drums and a guitar player with a guitar. They seated themselves. The preacher raised his arms and in a voice like a bass fiddle in low register said, "Let us pray."

He prayed for quite a while, as if God needed long assurance and supplication, while the pianist prayed to the piano, the guitarist to his guitar and the snare drummer to his waiting sticks.

Brother Sam called for music then, and the musicians played "Throw Out the Lifeline," played it in a kind of waiting tempo, as if celebration waited on the sinner's catching hold of the line.

Brother Sam thanked them and went into his spiel, as my father might have called it.

To hear Brother Sam tell it, we were all a bunch of miserable sinners, topers, adulterers, fornicators, unbelievers, name-in-vainers, gamblers, money changers. Our town was a nest of the ungodly.

Listening to him with half an ear, I thought we weren't so bad. We had our drunks, a couple of whom were in the tent, who repented every morning before the first drink. There was some sexual monkey business no doubt, but where wasn't there? Men gambled and used the name of the Lord in vain, meaning no disrespect. But, bar the murder that hadn't been solved, we were a pretty quiet and law-abiding community. I figured God could look on his handiwork without too much wrath, certainly not enough to consign us to the burning hell the preacher was talking about as if he'd seen it.

Having put us in our place, Brother Sam called for more music. The players, as if warmed by the sight of hell, put some warmth into

> I am a stranger here,
> Within a foreign land.
> My home is far away,
> Upon a golden strand.

Some of the hearers moved their feet to the beat.

The sun was setting on this tentful of sinners. With slow hands Brother Sam lit a couple of candles on the altar. Light and shadow played on his face.

Then he went into what my father had called the holy whine. His voice had a kind of chanting music in it. His mouth drew out the words it spoke. Come to Jesus, he was saying. Know the full love of God. Come to Jesus, all ye who are sore oppressed. Open your hearts to the heavenly light. Come to Jesus, who forgives the penitent. Repent, O sinners, repent. Be made new. And bless you, dear God. Bless these poor creatures who know not your love.

When Brother Sam ran out of steam, he borrowed some from the Bible. His words slurred and ran together. He was an auctioneer, auctioning salvation with an auctioneer's jabber.

There was a sway to the voice, and people swayed to it. They nodded, a good many did, and they listened, their faces intent, put under a spell, I had to remind myself, of hypnotic nonsense.

More music. This time it was "The Old-Time Religion,"
played as it never had been played in our Methodist
church. It was fast. It had a beat to it, a boogie beat, or
ragtime or jazz, that made feet and hands move. Brother
Sam sang, his voice big and true, and then nearly everyone joined in. The old-time religion. It was good enough
for father, you betcha. I told myself I was a deputy, not a
vocalist.

Afterwards Brother Sam made an embracing gesture.
Come forward, you who repent, he was saying. Come,
bend your heads, confess in prayer, and sweet Jesus, son
of God, will forgive you. Come forward ere the last curtain falls. Come. Come. Know peace. Know glory. Know
life everlasting.

A dozen or so of the audience did go forward and knelt
before the stage, and Brother Sam prayed for them. The
two chronic drunks were among them. It had been quite
a while between drinks.

The plate was being passed. The orchestra played
softly, as befit a sober moment. I contributed half a dollar,
thinking the evening worth it.

To my astonishment then, to my first-blush disbelief, I
saw a red head among the kneeling sinners, the head of
Red Fall.

In conclusion Brother Sam blessed us all, saved and
unsaved alike, and the people began to move out.

For no reason I could name I hung around while the
crowd thinned. I saw Red Fall talking to Brother Sam. I
saw Brother Sam put a kindly hand on his shoulder.

No disorder. No need for a town marshal. I went out a
tent flap and breathed God's air. Dark had fallen. As I took
the path to the footbridge, I heard steps behind me and

turned and made out the face of Red Fall. "A good meeting," he said as we walked along.

"Yeah. Quite a performance," I answered.

"Is that what you call it?" he asked.

What did he call it?

He had his reply on his tongue. "An inspiration."

Maybe I would have said more, but there was a slight rustling in the bushes beside the path, and by looking sharp I could make out a couple lying there.

Fall must have seen them, too, for after a few steps he said, "Disgusting. An abomination in the sight of God."

I answered, "Maybe so, but it's been going on for quite a while now."

"A stop should be put to behavior like that," he told me.

We had come to the footbridge and crossed it. "Better start with the preacher," I said.

"What do you mean?" There was an edge in his voice. "He is a man of God."

I let myself be sarcastic. "And doesn't know what his kind of excitement does to people?"

"That's enough," he said and angled away.

I went to the Commercial Cafe and asked Jessie Lou to bring me a hamburger. There were just three other customers, strangers to me. Revival meetings didn't seem to spur appetites, not for food, anyway.

"I'll be off in ten minutes, Jase," Jessie Lou said as she served me.

I said, "So?"

"I have something to tell you, if you can wait." Her eyes asked me to wait.

"Who wouldn't?" I answered, meaning to be just polite.

Later, after she had shucked her waitress outfit and we

were on the street, she said, "I have a little house, Jase, a house all to myself. Why don't we go there? I'll fix you a drink."

I asked, "Is it far? I have a car."

She took a quick hold on my arm. "No. Not in the police car. Please come on. Walk."

Her house, a little white thing on the south edge of town, looked neat. There was a flower garden in front of it, but the season was a little too early for blooms. She let us in with her key.

You couldn't call the inside elaborate, but it seemed comfortable enough. There were a lounge and small table and a couple of chairs in the living room, which had an old but clean carpet on it. Through an open door I could see a kitchen. A closed door must lead to her bedroom and bath.

The first thing Jessie Lou did after we entered was to pull down the blinds. Then she asked, "Bourbon and water? Sit down. Make yourself at home."

I said, "Thanks. Easy on the whiskey."

She went to the kitchen and brought back two drinks on a tray. I took mine, and, holding hers, she sat on a chair and faced me. "You have something to tell me?" I said.

She answered softly, "I guess you've heard, Jase?"

It struck me that she looked small and alone and sadder than a funeral flower. Pretty, though. Small-pretty and nicely built.

"How could I hear when you haven't told me?"

"I wasn't talking about that, but skip it for now." She took a slow sip from her glass and lifted her eyes to me. They appeared stricken. "I've always liked you, Jase."

"That's something. That's good," I said. "But I don't

know why. Two years ago you were too much of a kid for me. Sorry. You're not now. A couple of years make a difference. But we hardly knew each other except by name."

"I always looked up to you. That's why you're here now. Maybe I can help you, in your work, I mean."

"I hope so."

"There's that, and, besides, there's nobody else I can talk to. Nobody. About myself and my reasons. Oh, you'll hear about me soon enough, and that doesn't matter. But I'm a little afraid, Jase. It's foolish, maybe, and probably is. But squealing on somebody?"

"We don't go blabbing around, Jessie Lou. Nothing will come out that doesn't have to." I tried to smile. "Sheriff's orders."

She didn't continue. She sat, glass in hand, and looked at the walls as if, somehow, though they imprisoned her, she could see far beyond them, far beyond the walls and beyond hamburgers and French fries and fallen arches, could see a world dreamed about. I wanted to comfort her.

She left me to get two more drinks and sat silent again. I didn't speak. Whatever was on her mind would come out in time.

Finally and abruptly she said, "F. Y. Grimsley was laying Rosa Charlie."

I took a breath and asked, "Who says so? You can hear anything."

When she answered, I thought she was off the target. "I'm on the market, Jase." Her gaze went down as she spoke.

"In the market for what?"

Her face came up and seemed to implore me to understand. "I said *on* the market. I'm for sale."

"You don't—"

"Just what you think." As if I might suspect she was
propositioning me—which was possible—she added, "But
not to you, Jase. Not to you."

I still couldn't believe. I said, "You don't mean you're
selling it!"

"I have been. That's how I know about Grimsley and
Rosa. In bed a man tells things to a girl, especially if he's
half drunk."

I got up, my drink sloshing in my hand, and took a
couple of paces away, not seeing her now. She was a kid
even yet, barely of legal age if that, and she had been
putting out for money, lying with old bastards like Grimsley—and my world turned ugly on me.

"Good God!" I said. Out of the jumble of my mind a
stray thought turned up. "A man doesn't brag about fool-
ing around with another man's wife."

"It was a deal, Jase. Eagle Charlie knew."

I turned to face her, half-imagining she was somebody
else, some baggy old thing with pop eyes who had just one
thing to sell and it undesired. But she was still Jessie Lou,
young, pretty, forlorn—and, I thought, defiled.

It must have been my expression that brought a note of
defiance into her voice. She lifted her head, chin out, and
looked steadily at me. "Put yourself in my place if you can,
which I doubt. You're somebody. Your family is something. I'm nothing, and my family's not worth a damn.
The Whippett family. Just common trash."

I knew. Her father was a seasonal worker and sponger,
generally broke and drunk when he wasn't. Her mother

was a dreary woman who had given up long ago, that is if she had anything to give up. Her two brothers were louts.

"You don't have to be the same way," I said.

"I'm not going to be. That's the point. I'm one Whippett who's going to be able to hold her head up. I'm going to a secretarial school, probably in Spokane, and get away from my family and all."

My first astonishment, my first disbelief were gone now. In their place I felt only heaviness. "On money you make in bed?" I asked.

"On that and my pay and the tips I get. I have better than three hundred dollars saved up. I'll manage, and I'll say good-bye to the cafe and the town and my no-good family and my soiled reputation."

I stepped away from her again and then back. My father had fixed ideas about means and ends. I could hear him saying, "Don't expect good to come from bad, Jase. That's how politicians think, justifying bad actions in the name of noble ends that never turn out noble."

But now was no time for lectures, not to a girl who sat sad and defiant with far hope in her eyes. I said, "There must be another way, Jessie Lou, a better way."

"What?"

"I don't know. But you're a good girl, too good for what you're doing."

"Sure. I'm a Whippett. Don't you forget."

"You're yourself, and it's yourself I'm thinking of."

"Me, too. All the time." Her tone, like her words, had turned sharp. "You tell me no, but where's the yes to my life? Yes to the goddamn cafe. That's all you can say."

"I'm sorry."

She rose stiffly from her chair. "Good night."

She stepped to the door with me, and it wasn't until we reached there that I realized she was crying. I put an arm around her shoulder and kissed her without heat and said, "Remember, you're Jessie Lou, no one else, and you're a fine girl."

Chapter
Five

"WELL, if it ain't Hawkshaw himself," Halvor Amussen said the next morning. He had risen to greet me. He was big enough to eat hay.

"Hi, Mr. Town Marshal. Still the ladies' man, unless you've changed stripes, huh?" I answered. Over or through our talk I could hear voices in the inner office.

He held up the hand he had shaken mine with. It was the size of a college dictionary. "Cut it out, kid. I'm as good as married."

"Unlucky girl," I told him. "Back early, aren't you?"

"One day, more or less. What's the diff?"

"None, to a married man, I guess. High sheriff busy?"

"He said you could go in, favorite son."

"Your hinges squeak," I said.

I went into the inner office. Charleston sat at his desk. Seated opposite him was Dave Becker, who had his hat on, not in defiance but according to habit. His back was straight. I figured he was as promising of juice as a stone.

"You say that's all you know," Charleston was saying.

Becker replied, "Every bit."

I had brought pad and pencil with me and sat in a corner.

Charleston came forward in his chair, his eyes narrowed. "I don't believe you."

"If you wasn't sheriff, you wouldn't dast call me a liar."
I couldn't see Becker's face but knew it was closed and
harder than ever.

Charleston said, "You are, and I would, and I'll get the
facts out of you."

One of Becker's hands made a little gesture, as if saying,
"Just try it." Aloud, he answered, "Beat me to a frazzle
and wash out the frazzle, and you won't get what ain't
there."

Charleston got up, saying, "We'll see. And for your own
sake you'd better stay where I can get hold of you."

"Yes, sir, Mr. Sheriff," Becker answered, rising. "I'm
just a humble man and always go along with the law." His
bowlegs took him to the door. He let himself out.

Charleston sat down again. I went to the seat Becker
had left. "Tough citizen, out of tough country," he told
me. "Tonto Basin. Pleasant Valley. Heard about them?"

I answered I didn't.

"I dug it out of my mind last night, helped by a book,"
he said. "Range wars over sheep and cattle, they had
there. A long-lasting feud, too, the Graham-Tewksbury
feud. Both sides killed off, all but one. Zane Grey—you
know him?"

"Yes."

"He got the stuff for a book there. *To the Last Man.* The
ill wind blew him good, but nobody else."

"That wasn't in our time?" I asked. "Not in Becker's?"

"No. No close connection." He stopped for the right
words, which he could use when he wanted to. "But
remembered violence, a way of violence that gets cele-
brated by mouth or book—it colors a country for a long
time. Kids grow up with it in their bones. Anyhow, that's
the country Becker came from."

Charleston took one of his small daily quota of cigars and put a match to it. Through a puff of smoke he said, "Change of subject, Jase. Are your sins wiped clean?"

"No fault of Brother Sam's if they aren't. Ask Red Fall."

I told him about Fall then, and he said, "Hmm. Anything else to report?"

I had something all right, but I hesitated. Damn it, Jessie Lou was a good girl. Still, I had to say, "Grimsley was laying Rosa Charlie, Eagle's wife."

"You seem to speak with considerable authority. How come you know, Jase?"

There was nothing else for it then. I gave him what I had learned.

He sighed, his face showing concern and regret. He said, "That seems authentic enough." He paused and added quietly, "I knew about Jessie Lou."

"I feel sorry for her. I like her regardless."

His eyes rose to mine. "I can tell that you do." He looked down at his desk. "She's not the first girl who has thought to elevate herself by her tail. Sorry doings, boy."

"She said she was a little afraid to tell me. She talked about what happened to squealers."

"No grounds for fear. Hell, who cares? Grimsley's dead, and Eagle Charlie was in on the deal for Rosa. No trouble for Jessie Lou. Reassure her."

I said that I would, knowing the truth when I heard it.

"All right. To business," Charleston said, leaning forward. "Would you recommend seeing Rosa Charlie? You want to quiz her yourself?"

The question brought me up in my chair. "Good Lord, Mr. Charleston, I couldn't do that!"

Charleston removed his cigar. A small smile touched his

mouth. "Of course not, Jase. I wouldn't suggest it seriously. You've been acting so down in the spirit, I wanted to see if there was any life left. I see there is."

He snubbed out his half-smoked cigar, got up and put on his silver-gray hat. "I said, to business. Bring your pad, Jase."

I said, "Sure, but could I ask where?"

He ushered me toward the door. "We're going to see Eagle Charlie, who else?"

The land lay greening and peaceful, young land, I thought, in the young season. Later, wheat would ripen and the grasses stand ready for the cutter bar, but now was the time of growth, of soil and seed hope. The road dipped and curved and climbed toward the foothills that would climb into mountains. The picket pin gophers were out, some mere babies, and Charleston, silent, tried to keep from running them over. He couldn't avoid all of them. When, in spite of his efforts, he flattened one, he shook his head. Another rider would have thought he was too softhearted for the office of sheriff.

Short of Grimsley's place, he turned right into a road less traveled. He asked, "Ever been to Breedtown, Jase?"

"Not since I was a boy," I told him. "I was kind of scared of the place then. All those Indians."

"Yep, but no need to be. I don't guess it's Indians so much as the sight of poverty that people shy away from. Poverty has an ugly face, and so we tend to think it's the face of the red man because it lives with him. But whoa, boy, on this sociology talk. We're officers of the law."

"Yes, sir."

We topped a rise, and in the near distance I saw a

scatter of buildings. You could call them buildings, that is, if you counted sagging log cabins and slab-built shacks. They sat out from a double log cabin which had a garden by it. We forded a trickle of stream from what must be Eagle Charlie's spring and pulled up by a door.

There were mothers and kids around some of the shacks and more lean curs than I took time to count. The dogs loped to the car, barking tenor and bass. I like dogs all right, but don't like to get bitten. Charleston left the car, paying no heed, and I got out, too, paying heed.

Charleston knocked at what seemed to be the main door. I wasn't prepared for what came to answer it. Good Lord, she was beautiful, beautiful as only young part-blood girls get, and then only rarely. Her hair was black, her eyes big, her features fine, her skin tinged with copper. Over her shoulders she wore a piece of red blanket. She had on worn jeans and a man's old shirt. The body they clothed must have been born in the wild, she seemed that fine-boned and graceful.

Charleston asked, "Mrs. Charlie?"

She nodded. Behind the delicate curve of her lips her teeth showed white in a half-smile.

"I'd like to speak to Eagle Charlie, if he's around."

I think it was then that she noticed Charleston's badge, for the smile left her face, and she said, "Policemen?"

"Sheriff," Charleston answered. "But don't be alarmed. I thought maybe Charlie could help me."

Without answering, she stepped back and withdrew, on her face as she turned an expression of troubled wonder.

She had left the door open for us while she disappeared through an entrance. The room we walked into was habit-

able but no more than that. An old Majestic range occupied most of one end. Out from it were a table and three
chairs of sorts, standing on worn linoleum. A couple of
sawed wooden blocks apparently served as chairs, too.
Some cast-iron cooking utensils hung from the wall near
the range. A water bucket with dipper sat on a rough
bench. The place was clean. We waited.

I had never seen Eagle Charlie, or, if I had, I couldn't
remember. He came through the door, a short, square-
built man with a striking thatch of hair that had turned
mostly white. He was, I thought, too damn old for his wife,
even if his face would have adorned a coin, not a nickel
but a sure-enough silver dollar.

Charleston shook hands with him and introduced me.
Eagle Charlie motioned to the blocks, and we sat down.
Before anyone spoke again, I heard a door close and con-
cluded that Rosa Charlie had left the cabin.

"We are asking questions that might put us on the track
of the man who murdered F. Y. Grimsley," Charleston
said.

Eagle Charlie answered, "Too bad."

"What's too bad, Charlie?" Charleston asked. "That he
got killed or that we're trying to find out who killed him?"

From that classic Indian face came, "Him dead."

"Yes, he's dead. How come? Any idea? Got a hunch?"

"Me, him friends. Good friends," Eagle Charlie said.
"Too bad him dead. How?" He shook his head in answer
to his own question. "Dead is all."

Charleston leaned forward, and a hand came out. One
finger on it jabbed at Eagle Charlie. "Stop that fake Indian
talk, Charlie. Speak plain!"

Eagle Charlie smiled a wide smile, which didn't hurt his

appearance one bit. "English? French? Piegan?" he asked.

"English will do. You have no idea as to the murder, no information, no suspicion, no leads at all?"

"My head, he's empty."

"Empty, huh? Not that empty. Your wife was having dates with Grimsley."

Not a flicker appeared in the dark eyes, not a twitch in the cheeks. The mouth said, "So?"

"What's more, you knew about it. You traded her off for money or, more likely, a beef now and then."

"So?"

"So maybe you fell out. Maybe you conked him. Don't give me that 'so' again."

"So maybe not. Me, him friends, I tell you. Grimsley give me a beef sometimes." It was plain now that Charlie wouldn't forsake his brand of language, fake or not.

"In trade?"

Eagle Charlie smiled that wide smile again. He thrust both hands out, fingers spread. It occurred to me that he was enjoying himself.

"No, my friend, no," he was saying. "No trade. Sure, once a week, maybe, she see him. She always come back. Beef never go back. No trade then, see? She same woman as before, so why not? Same woman, I say, and all the time Charlie's squaw, and we have meat in the pot. Savvy? Why not?"

Charleston looked at him and looked at me. "A real businessman, Jase." Then he turned back to Charlie. "Did you make her whore with anyone else?"

"I no make her do one thing. Whore? No. All right with her, all right with me, good for Grimsley, good for us."

Charleston rose from the block with nothing showing in his face. "Come on, Jase." Eagle Charlie smiled us good-bye.

Outside, women and children and a couple of men were pretending not to be interested. Among them was a sure-enough squaw, a pureblood who seemed close to a hundred years old. The eyes in her ancient face glinted with wisdom or hatred or maybe indifference. The snarling dogs hurried me into the car.

Once we had crossed the little creek, Charleston said, "What do you make of him, Jase?"

"He was putting on a show."

"Oh, sure. He knows English as well as most men, and he knew we knew it. He was laughing at us. But what else?"

I said, "I can't figure him. What kind of a man trades his wife off that way?"

"He does, for one. And he probably thinks he's getting the best of the deal. The goods he trades—his wife, I mean —he gets back, undamaged according to his lights. But he keeps and eats the meat. Neat trick on the white man."

Charleston allowed me a little time to think, then went on. "I would guess he's a sly character, Jase. Just consider. For the most part, around here, nearly everyone with Indian blood in him is regarded as a little less than human, nearly everybody but Eagle Charlie. He's pretty much accepted. He laughs and jokes with the boys and gets slapped on the shoulder and takes his turn buying drinks."

"What's wrong with that?"

"Nothing. But I bet if he could get away with it he'd play dirty with any white man and count it an Indian victory. It may be all an act, this palsy-walsy business."

"Play dirty? Including murder?" I asked.

"I didn't say that."

"What do you say then?"

He answered, "Pisswillie."

Chapter
Six

IT WAS MID-MORNING of the next day when Charleston and I set out for Guy Jamison's ranch.

The office had been full-staffed when I reached there earlier, Jimmy and Halvor both being on hand, and Charleston, too, in the inner office. I asked Halvor, mostly to make conversation, "How was the show last night?"

He shook his head, as if some roll of thought made him do it. "The man's got something, Hawkshaw. You can't deny it."

"Yea, Brother Sam!" Jimmy said. "All aboard on the glory train."

"Not with you on it," Halvor told him. "What do you know about him, anyway? Nothin', so shut up."

I said, "I guess Red Fall has a ticket."

"What if he has?" Halvor asked. "Never knock a believer, you two. A man's got a right to believe, and who says it don't help him? Think on that. The preacher's got something, I tell you."

I didn't answer, thinking what Brother Sam had was a slick way of selling salvation to suckers. It beat me that a man like Halvor would buy it. He had the morals of a tomcat until his intended put a leash on him, and here he was mewing for heaven instead of the alley. I think I felt a little sad for him.

I went into the inner office. Charleston put down the paper he had been glancing at. "Want to make a thousand dollars, Jase?" he asked.

"Any time, depending."

"No strings. Just find out who killed F. Y. Grimsley."

"Who pays?"

"It's solid enough. The Stockmen's Association. Reward money posted."

"Kind of stingy, isn't it?"

"Generous enough, since nobody liked him."

He tapped the letter with a forefinger. "There are a couple of stipulations."

My eyes asked him what.

"First off, I'm to determine the winner, no one else. No advice and consent from the county commissioners, no approval by the stockmen themselves. I'm judge and jury."

"How will that set with the commissioners?"

He shrugged. "No skin off us. Politics in action, Jase. Opposite parties. The stockmen are mostly Republican."

Charleston was an independent, largely supported by both parties. As if to enforce what I knew, he smiled and said, "So they tap a eunuch."

"You said two stipulations?"

"Next, the reward must go to an individual, not to this office or any other agency, public or private."

"What about you? What about any deputy? All out of the running?"

"Nope. Not specified, but leave me out." He smiled again. "Pretty picture—the judge and jury rewarding himself."

Charleston got up. "You have yesterday's report to

type?" When I nodded, he went on, "I have to see the treasurer and the county commissioners. Then what say we ride out to Guy Jamison's?"

Now, riding along, I asked, "Why Jamison in particular?"

"Nothing particular about it. Straw in the water to grab at. Might be he could tell us something about his dude wrangler."

"Those red hairs you found—?"

I thought his head moved a little, sidewise. "Who knows, Jase? Seems like a long-distance maybe."

That was that, it seemed. He wasn't going to tell me any more.

It didn't matter. The day did, a nice day, the rare day in June. The sun rode high and just warm enough, and along the banks of the Rose River to our left the cottonwoods and aspens had a green-hold on hope. I got a sniff of chokecherry in bloom. And there were always the mountains, shining clear now, four miles away and as near as the windshield. But for them, it struck me, my eye would see the coasts of Japan. The nearer peaks were only snow-patched but the farther ones cloaked in almost unbroken white.

To our right a gravel lane led to Charleston's upland home, which he didn't own but his father-in-law did. The father-in-law was off, as usual, on some geological expedition, this time in Arizona, so I had heard. Charleston had a special phone at the place and kept his little apartment in the Jackson Hotel for nights when things were hot.

Charleston turned into the lane, saying, "I'll just tell Geet." He smiled. "Who knows, she might have some lunch for us later."

As he braked, he said, "Just a minute." He got out. Geet had come to the door. They embraced as if they hadn't seen each other since the presidential election. Once, two years ago, I had been stuck on that girl, but just in a moony way. Charleston was the man for her.

When he came back, he said with a smile, "Geet thinks she may be able to scrape up something."

We rolled into the Rose River canyon, and the mountains folded us in, only to draw back a couple of miles farther on and allow for a natural park on which Jamison had put up his buildings. A couple of new cabins, neat as neat could be, had been constructed since I was there last. An artist with both wood and metal, Jamison was doing something in his tool shed when we stopped. "Got a minute, Guy?" Charleston called.

Jamison flicked off some kind of saw, let go a piece of wood and walked out to us. "Sure thing," he said. He gave us a good hand and smile. "Go on up to the house. See you in a minute."

We gathered in the lodge room after Guy had introduced us to his wife's grandpa, whose name I didn't catch. The old man was in a wheelchair, sucking on a pipe that he had to hold with his hand for lack of teeth. He was drooling a little on his age-puckered chin, but his eyes were as bright as a chipmunk's. "The wife's gone to town," Jamison told us. Then, "Everything all right, Grandpa?"

Grandpa answered, "Why not?" and pulled on the pipe, which had gone out.

To us Jamison said, "Cook watches out for him when we're not around. He pinches her butt if she doesn't take care. Don't you, old pardner?"

Grandpa answered, "What'd you say? You, Guy, isn't it?"

"Off and on," Guy told us. "He's a game old rooster, though." He offered us beer, which we turned down in favor of coffee.

Once we were sipping it, Charleston said, "You know about Grimsley, of course?"

"I haven't been to town. Mail just twice a week until later. What little I know came from the radio. Got his head beat in, didn't he?"

"Right. He was found dead on his back stoop by his man, Dave Becker. No clues yet."

"You could suspect practically everyone in the county, including me."

"Becker, too?"

"Who knows? I can't guess."

I had my book out but wasn't taking notes yet. The cook, who was running to fat, appeared at the door to the kitchen and looked the situation over. She padded up and lit a match for Grandpa's pipe, being careful to keep her rear in the rear.

"So a lot of people are suspect," Charleston went on after she had disappeared. "The day before Grimsley was murdered, he was raising hell about his stock being rustled. He pointed us—the office, that is—toward Breedtown. He was wondering, too, about Luke McGluke. Know him?"

"To see. You have to see him to believe it. Not the murder. The man."

"It seems he spends some time at Breedtown. At least Grimsley said so."

"Maybe so. I don't know."

Charleston put his cup in the saucer and went on. "You got a young fellow here, working, name of Red Fall."

"Working off and on until later. But what in hell brings him up?"

Charleston shook his head. "Not him more than others. What can you tell me?"

"I met him at a dude ranchers' convention. He wanted work. He had the references. I hired him."

"And?"

"I haven't had much for him to do. He shod the horses and mules, all of them. Good job, too. He put the gear in working order. No complaint at all, not from me or him. He'll come back when the first party of dudes arrives, or maybe a day or two before then."

"No trouble with him? Gambling? Drinking?"

"Good God, no! Not one bit. And polite and clean-spoken. Doesn't swear or like to hear others swear. I tell you, he takes his religion straight, old-fashioned, fundamental, absolute."

I wasn't aware that Grandpa was listening until he spoke in his broken voice. "Ha. Ha. Give me a son of a bitch any time.'

Jamison said easily, "Now, Grandpa, you don't know anything about him."

"My light's gone out," the old man said, waving his pipe as if it were to blame.

Jamison got up, saying, "So your light's out." He took the pipe, knocked it out in an ashtray, filled it from a Prince Albert can, gave it back and scratched a match, holding it while Grandpa puffed.

Seated again, Jamison said, "Breedtown." He paused before he spoke again. "My man, Red, goes there quite often, I understand." He waited for a response and, getting none, added, "Don't get the wrong idea, though."

"What's the right one?"

"Among other things he's a student. Interested, anyhow, in the beliefs, the superstitions, the old tribal stories of Indians."

"Yes?" Charleston said.

"There's a pureblood squaw there, a crone, old as time. I guess she's Eagle Charlie's mother. He talks to her, takes notes, I believe."

"Talks? In English, Blackfoot? What?"

"I don't know. Through an interpreter, maybe. I don't imagine she understands his language or he understands hers. I just can't tell you."

Charleston was fiddling with a cigar. "You kind of vouch for this man?"

"From what I know of him, yes. I like his work. He's dependable. He knows horses."

"You know his background?"

"Mostly from his references. He's worked in Arizona and New Mexico. Raised somewhere down there, I suppose. But, Chick, what makes you suspect him? I ask again."

"Did I say I did?"

"All these questions. Is it just because he's a newcomer?"

There was no heat in Jamison's words and none in Charleston's reply. "I bark up a lot of wrong trees, Guy, but I have to ask, foolish or not."

Charleston got to his feet. So did Jamison and I. Jamison said, "Yeah, I know, Chick. I guess I know."

Before we reached the door, Grandpa got hold of

Charleston's sleeve with one hand. The pipe in the other jabbed toward me. To Charleston he said, "Watch out for that Jesus Christ."

Behind us Jamison murmured, "Grandpa. Now, Grandpa."

We drove back and took Charleston's turn-in. Geet was ready for us, with ham sandwiches, tuna fish, milk, coffee and pie. Married life agreed with her, I thought as I ate. She was more comely—my dad's word—than even I remembered.

As we were finishing, she asked, "I hope you'll be back tonight, Chick?"

"Barring an act of God," he answered. In his circumstances I doubted even an act of God could keep me in town. He wiped his mouth, rose, kissed her and said to me, "Let's go, J.C."

Quite a promotion, from Hawkshaw to J.C. I would have to ask Halvor to show more respect.

Chapter Seven

As we approached town that afternoon, Charleston said to me, "I'm going to drop you off, Jase. See if you can round up Framboise and Pete Pambrun. Not likely they're working. Bring them to the office."

I asked, "How?"

His teeth showed in a grin. "You figure it out. That's what deputies are for—to do the sheriff's thinking."

He dropped me off in front of the Bar Star, raised his hand in a cheerful good-bye and headed down for the office.

I stood outside for a minute or two. How to get those two men to the office? Not by a show of authority. They weren't suspects, not yet. They would high-tail it if I acted bossy and didn't charge them because I couldn't. Buy them a few drinks, then, and cozen them into a visit? Nope. White man buy firewater for poor Injun? Nope. They didn't look so dumb. They'd see through my generosity. Let inspiration visit me, Brother Sam.

I entered the Bar Star. Only Tad Frazier was there, reading a newspaper and picking his teeth while he waited for customers. He raised the toothpick in salute.

"Good place to start a saloon," I told him.

"Yeah. It just might make out, but not if every day was like today."

"Maybe everyone's got religion. Maybe that tent preacher is bobtailing your business."

"Naw," Tad said. "Crap. He makes people thirsty. Too bad for us tonight's his last night."

I knew I was killing time, not wanting to come up against Framboise and Pambrun. "Break the drouth and draw me a beer," I said. I didn't want the beer. "Have one yourself."

He answered he would.

I didn't ask about the two breeds. If word got out that I was looking for them, they'd be long gone. Instead I asked, "You have any hunches about who killed one Grimsley?"

"Sure. I did. I gave him one of my poison looks, and it took. But why ask me? Better I ask you. You're the law and smart."

"Thanks. Not smart, though. Not smart enough."

Tad said, "What does it matter?"

"It matters a thousand dollars."

"Too much. A nickel would be about right."

I said, "See you later," and went out, leaving half my beer.

The Club Pool Hall stood at a diagonal across the street. It was called a pool hall because it had one table in it, never used and hardly usable, its felt torn by forgotten players who had miscued. Its attractions were soft drinks, beer and low-stake card games, rum and pitch mostly. Old men frequented it, and younger ones with only a few nickels in their jeans. I decided to have a look.

My men weren't there, either of them, and after watching a slow game at one of the two occupied tables I went back out, wondering where to go next.

I lagged down the street, looking for cars that just might have the beat-up mark of Breedtown on them. Three or four clunkers were parked at the curbs, but none told me anything. My idea was dumb anyhow.

Mike Day was taking the air in front of the bank, as was the right and privilege of the owner. He said, "Good afternoon, Jase. What's on your mind?"

In approaching him I had to step over one of his setters, which asked mildly what was my business. "Murder," I said, shaking the hand he put out.

"Yes. Too bad. It gives a man to think."

I asked, "What are you thinking?" I was sure of an answer. Day had ideas about everything.

"Young man, I'm afraid you and the sheriff—no disrespect—are just chasing your tails. You quiz the wrong people, probably put the wrong questions."

"How do you know that? From talking to Eagle Charlie or Becker or somebody?"

"I hear things. Who doesn't? I'm here to tell you Becker's a solid man."

"I didn't say he wasn't. You have something to suggest? We could use a tip or two."

His gaze left mine, looking at the case with a banker's eye. "Grimsley wasn't killed for personal gain. No sense in that. No love angle, either. It was an enemy killed him," he said.

"We already figured that out ourselves."

"Forget the locals. Look afar, Jason. Look afar. Grimsley had business contacts way beyond county limits. Inquire into them. It's a cinch he gypped some stranger who returned the trick in blood." Day looked pleased with his language. "He was that kind of a man." Now he spoke with such force that one of his setters opened an eye to see what was the matter. "Hell, he didn't even bank in town. How's that for loyalty?"

I left him with his thoughts about loyalty.

It was getting along toward late afternoon. I went home and practiced the fingerprinting I had neglected for a couple of years and studied the book the FBI had sent at my request.

At supper my father said, "Thank God, that evangelist is striking his tent after tonight."

Thinking of Halvor, I said, "I guess he's made some converts."

"Who'll revert the minute he turns his back if not sooner. Infernal nonsense!"

I had more important things on my mind, so I told my parents about my problem—how to get Framboise and Pambrun to the sheriff's office. "What's the trick?" I asked. "What's the approach? I've racked my brain and come up with nothing."

Mother said with a mother's smile, "You'll find a way, Jason."

My father studied his plate and then looked at me and spoke with the certainty of old conviction. "Candor, son," he said. "Complete candor. Men answer to it. No tricks. No deception whatever. State your purpose honestly, openly. They're breeds, some would say, but breeds are human, for goodness' sake, even if they're not always treated that way. Be candid."

I said, "All right and thanks. Now I have to find them."

I couldn't, though, even though I looked until bedtime and past. But I did find a reason.

The evangelist had sung his last chant just before I

dropped into the Bar Star. I knew he had because automobile lights were coming from the direction of the tent. They began casting beams along the deserted street. Foot travelers would be following soon. A dull game was in progress at the Bar Star. The players were the only customers besides a drunk who was dozing at the end of the bar. Bob Studebaker, the owner, had relieved Tad Frazier as bartender.

I was tired of pretending I was looking for nobody. And, having failed so far, how I could fail more by asking. "Bob," I said, moving up to the bar, "have Pete Pambrun or Framboise showed up tonight?"

He plunged a couple of glasses in wash water, dried his hands and answered, or, rather, didn't. "Looking for them, huh?"

"Now what would make you think that?"

"Easy as shit. You asked."

"Well. Have they?"

He leaned his bare, plump forearms on the bar. "Would you expect them to?"

"Why not? You're not on their blacklist."

"You got a lot to learn, Jase."

I said, "Tell me."

"No breeds in town today. Nobody from Breedtown. Why? Because they know they'll be grilled. They figure they're suspects, being part war-whoop. That's why. That's the goddamn why. You're anti-business, you and Chick Charleston. Have a drink."

"No, thanks."

"Buy one then, seeing as how I wised you up."

"On duty, Bob. Later, you can bet."

We were smiling at each other, smiling honest smiles.

I walked to the Commercial Cafe, feeling hungry, though God knew Mother had fed me enough. A gang of teenagers occupied a table, noisy and drippy with the ketchup they drowned their hamburgers in.

I asked Jessie Lou for a ham sandwich and coffee. She didn't meet my eyes, either in taking the order or filling it. Had she, I guess I would have looked down.

On the way home I thought: Another day lost.

Chapter
Eight

I WENT to the office early the next morning, before anyone but Jimmy Conner was there. "I need the keys to the
county car," I told him. "Be in later."

"I can't be givin' out keys without orders," he answered. "Who says give you one? Better wait around until
the sheriff shows up."

You had to make allowances for a man probably just out
of bed. You had to indulge old, old-time employees who
got to thinking they were essential to operations. Besides,
I liked Jimmy.

"Aw, quit it, Jimmy," I said, giving him a big smile. "You
know me. I'm Jason Beard, if you've forgotten. Remember? I chase up to the Commercial Cafe and bring grub
to your guests in the crowbar house and so save you walking. If I go now, I'll be back in time to do that chore for
you."

He looked down. "My goddamn feet. Get the key yourself," he said, needlessly pointing to the key hook. As I left,
he added, "Good luck with whatever it is."

So here I was on the road to Breedtown, bent on bring-
ing Pete Pambrun and Framboise to the office for questioning.

The day was raw. A gale blew out of the canyons to the

west. I could almost see the air massing in the mountains and charging out on command. God's command, I supposed Brother Sam would have said. The car swerved and lurched in the face of it, and the steering wheel tried to spin from my hands. June, the Moon of the Wild Rose, by the old Indian calendar. It might better have been named the Moon of the Wild Winds. What rose would blossom in this weather? What did blossom was dust and the pebbles that peppered the car.

But somehow it was my wind. The mountains were mine and the whipped country that waited good days. There was the sure if suffering hope in it, and I wondered if all men came to look on their birthplaces, however stricken, as home.

In an English class I had tried to put my feelings for place, for my place, on paper, but the words came out flat or florid, and I gave up and hugged the feeling to myself.

It was a mistake to let my thoughts ramble away from the road. I missed the churned track and got stuck at the ford across Eagle Charlie's little spring stream. The back wheels spun in the mud and wash gravel and ground deeper as I fed gas to the engine.

I was close to the settlement, just a hundred yards or so away from it, but no one watched that I could see and no one came out to help. One cur, its hair fluttered and flattened by the wind, added a couple of barks to the shrill voice of it. I had to put my shoulder against the door of the car to get out. It slammed shut behind me. I got my boots muddy on the shore of the stream.

In the leeward shelter of a corner stood Eagle Charlie and the old Indian woman I had seen before. The dark of her face looked darker with rage. Her mouth twisted with talk, and her eyes were black as aimed gun barrels. I caught the hoarse gutturals of Indian speech. An edge of wind hit one of her braids. It stood out from her head like a spike of feeling. Eagle Charlie said something and made a sweep with one hand and arm as if to brush her away. Turning, he saw me and nodded.

I asked where I could find Framboise and Pambrun. He pointed to a shack toward my left, saying nothing.

He and she were the only people in sight. The rest, I supposed, were walled up against the wind. A board tore loose from an eave and made a shudder of sound like a thrown shingle. Somehow a couple of tepees managed to hold themselves upright. Outside the shack a saddle horse stood, reins trailing, rump to the gale, which tore at mane and tail and the short hair of haunch.

The shack was partly log, badly notched. Its roof was weathered board. One plank lifted and sank and lifted again at the wind's urging.

My knock got the answer "What do you want?"

"To come in, first of all."

"No lock on the door."

It was a single-room shack. The room was thick with human smell and the odor of tobacco, but it was tidy beyond expectation. The worn wooden floor was swept clean, and not a cobweb hung from walls or roof, none that I could see at first glance. Pambrun—it turned out to be—sat on a made bed. Framboise occupied a battered chair held together by haywire. A bucket and pitcher stood on a bench near a midget cookstove over which kitchenware hung.

I said, "Hi. How are you?"

The answer was noises in the throats.

"That wind's a bastard today."

The report wasn't news to them.

"Could I talk to you a while?" I asked.

They looked at each other. Framboise said, "Talk away. It's free." He was a big man, broad-faced, with so dark a complexion as to make a man wonder if some female ancestor hadn't got mixed up with the black man who accompanied Lewis and Clark.

"The sheriff would like to see you."

Pambrun answered, "We're here." He was a thin, small man, lighter of skin than the other.

"He's trying to find out who killed Grimsley. He thought you might help."

"Why pick on us?" Framboise said.

Pambrun replied to him, "Because we're goddamn Injun."

"You're wrong there," I said. "We're not picking on anybody. We're just asking questions."

Pambrun said, "No answers here. Not a damn answer."

"And damn if we go to town," Framboise put in.

Uninvited, I took a seat on a sawed block that apparently served as one.

"Look," I said. "Let's keep it friendly. I know you by sight. You know me. I'm a deputy. My name's Jason Beard."

Their eyes met again. "Beard?" Pambrun said to the other.

"One they call Bill."

They both nodded their heads in secret agreement.

"Bill Beard is my father," I said.

They studied me slowly as if to find signs of my ancestry.

"You as good a man as he is?" Pambrun asked. Except that his lips moved, his face was a blank.

"No," I replied, "but I try to be."

Pambrun said, "Beard" again. Then neither spoke.

I scrambled in my mind. How open them up? "It was my father's idea," I said, though it wasn't, "that I bring a drink for our meeting." I dug in my windbreaker and brought out a flask I had bought.

"It's a trick, huh? Soften us up. No?"

His gaze was on Pambrun, who said, "Not Beard. Not Bill Beard. No."

"No."

Their eyes quickened then. Pambrun got up. I handed him the bottle. He went to a shelf and found tin cups, poured whiskey into each and watered the whiskey from the bucket. The cups were clean. Taking mine, I felt like a cheat and a traitor. Sure, I wanted to soften them up and so had resorted to the white trader's oldest trick, helped, I didn't know why, by the name of my father.

Settled again, Pambrun said, "Honest to God, we don't know a thing."

"But just the same, ask away," Framboise told me.

I wished Charleston were there. He would know the right questions. I said, "Were Grimsley and Eagle Charlie friends?"

"Maybe," Pambrun replied after taking a swallow. "They got along, anyhow."

"Why in hell should Eagle Charlie wipe him out?" Framboise added. "Dead, Grimsley is no use to him."

"But he was before then?"

They considered, their eyes meeting.

Pambrun said, "Every once in a while Eagle Charlie got a free beef. He divvied it up. We all got some."

"Free for what?" I had a sudden but passing notion to

dig into the subject of Rosa Charlie and her assignations with Grimsley.

Pambrun shrugged and began building a cigarette. "I hear, once long ago, that hungry Indians butchered cows they didn't own."

"But no more?"

"No more. Not us. People think so, but Eagle Charlie would kick us off."

"He was still a son of a bitch, that Grimsley," Framboise said. "Who cares he's dead?"

Pambrun looked at me, a question in his face as he fiddled with his empty cup. I bobbed my head, and he made more drinks.

The information I was getting was pretty old stuff, so I changed the subject. "That Luke McGluke—you know him—he comes around, doesn't he?"

With his finger Framboise drew circles around his temple. "He comes. Sometimes he brings grub, a little. No harm."

"What about the man named Red Fall? You've seen him here."

It was Pambrun who answered. "He talks to the old squaw. He likes old stories, old Indian ways, old what you call beliefs."

"Does she talk English?"

"She can, but she won't," Framboise replied. "Not a word. Makes believe not to savvy."

"But Fall, can he understand her?"

"Rosa helps out."

"Oh," I said, "you mean she interprets?"

They nodded, both of them.

"The old woman," I asked, "is Eagle Charlie's mother?"

"No," Framboise replied. "Rosa's grandma."

"They don't like each other, not from what little I've seen?"

"That old one is tough," Pambrun said in his turn. "They fight all the time."

"What about?"

"Anything. For her there is too much white man in Eagle Charlie. She lives in the long ago." He paused and went on, "She's a good Catholic."

"Old Indian, a blanket squaw you might say, and still a good Catholic. That's kind of strange."

Pambrun said, "No. The priests raised her. But the priests, they were pretty wise. With Indians, I mean. The Indians thought one way, the priests another, but the priests let them mix. What the hell? Not so different."

Framboise broke in. "What's that got to do with Grimsley? The old one and Eagle Charlie can't get along. So what?"

I had to grin at him and answer, "You're right. I'm off the track. Have another drink. Not for me, thanks."

Pambrun attended to the two cups.

I said, "I don't think the sheriff will need to see you," and felt sure he wouldn't. "I'm satisfied, for now, anyhow. Thanks for the talk, and so long."

They both got up as Framboise said, "Going, huh?" A smile, the first one, came to his ugly face. "Going out to spin your wheels, huh?"

So they knew I was stuck, as probably everyone in the settlement did. Framboise motioned to Pambrun and the two came out the door with me, leaving their unfinished drinks. The wind had died to a breeze.

Pambrun went to the drooping horse and got a rope

from the saddle. Framboise tightened the cinch. Pambrun went to his knees and tied one end of the rope to my axle, walked back and gave the other end to Framboise, who had mounted. I climbed in the car and started the engine. Framboise took a couple of dallies around the saddle horn and kicked the horse into motion.

With the horse pulling and my hind wheels grabbing for traction, it didn't take long to get out of the mud.

After untying the rope from the axle Pambrun had gone back into the shack. He returned and offered me the half-empty bottle.

"Keep it with my thanks," I said.

Again their glances met, and then Pambrun said, "Say how to your father."

Chapter
Nine

OVER SAUSAGE and buckwheat pancakes I asked my father, "How is it you're friends with two characters named Pete Pambrun and Framboise? I don't know what his first name is."

Mother was at the stove frying more cakes.

Father said, "Louis."

"But how come?"

"Simple. Soon after you left town."

I waited for him to take, chew and swallow a bite.

"It was your late friend, Grimsley," he said.

"That explains everything, does it?"

"Why don't you let your father finish his breakfast, Jase?" Mother asked me.

Father smiled and said, "Never mind. I'm about through." He helped himself to more pancakes. There was nothing for me to do except sit and eat.

At last Father said, "Grimsley accused those two men of rustling a steer. Trumped-up evidence, but he pretty well convinced the county attorney that he had a case. Halvor Amussen, your sidekick, too. Mr. Charleston was on vacation, and Amussen was in charge of the office—too much in charge."

"Even then, Grimsley was out to get the breeds?"

"Right, but I guess there's no doubt that he'd lost a steer or two, maybe more."

"He hadn't accused anybody since then, no one except just before he got clobbered?"

Mother, having seated herself, said, "That sounds unfeeling and vulgar, Jase."

Father waved her comment away. "He learned a lesson that didn't last long enough."

"Tell me."

"I knew Framboise and Pambrun couldn't be guilty. I said so."

"You know your father," Mother said.

I asked, "How did you know?"

"Because I saw them. I went fishing up the Rose River canyon and saw them. They had pitched a tent there. They were cutting and trimming logs to bring out and fishing a little themselves. They said they had been there for four days and probably would spend three or four more."

"You took their word for it?"

"Not entirely. I saw the prepared logs. To me they spelled out work, considerable work. I saw the camp. It obviously had been pitched there some time. I saw how they'd got there and would leave—in an antique lumber wagon drawn by an old team of horses that couldn't travel two miles an hour. All this at the very time the steer was supposed to have been stolen."

"Why didn't you tell me before?" I asked.

Mother answered, "It takes a lot of talking to make up for two years, Jase."

"It just didn't occur to me," Father said.

"So what next?"

"I ran into Framboise and Pambrun in town. They were scared. They knew they were about to be charged. I went to the county attorney with them and told what I knew for a fact. Nothing ever came of it."

"You don't mean of what you said?"

"No. The charge. It never was made. Case dropped. Trumped-up evidence, that's all it was. We scotched it."

Again Mother said, "You know your father."

"I don't know what I know," I replied. "Charleston never told me, either."

Father smiled. "I understand."

"I don't."

"Then you don't really know Mr. Charleston. Look, son, Amussen is all right, I suppose, but no one ever accused him of being extra smart. Mr. Charleston didn't want to prejudice you. He wanted you to find out for yourself."

I was still thinking about those words as I left for the office.

Charleston listened to my report about Pambrun and Framboise, which I hadn't been able to make the previous afternoon because he was out of the office.

At the end he asked, "Pick up anything else?"

"Only the idea that Eagle Charlie and that old blanket squaw—maybe you've seen her—don't get along. She's Rosa's grandma."

"Old Woman Gray Wolf, they call her. Tough old girl. Hates whites. I tried to talk to her once. No luck. I have an idea she talks mostly to her ancestors and maybe the priest."

"She was talking to Eagle Charlie, talking hot, or I miss my guess. I don't know why."

For a minute Charleston was silent, as if letting a theory

take shape. "In the old tribal days," he said, "a husband could and often did loan his squaw out, for friendship or money. She could sleep with another man, but only with the consent of the husband. Common thing and considered moral enough. But Rosa's grandma hates whites and hates Charlie's association with them. Then for him to trade Rosa to Grimsley, a white man! I can see it wouldn't set well with her. Sounds reasonable, huh?"

"I suppose so. She was bound to know, I would think."

Charleston rose from his chair. "Everything seems in hand, everything but the murder. Court's sitting, and I have to appear in a couple of pisswillie cases. Take the afternoon off, though you better call in a couple of times just to check. I want you to get on the tail of that Luke McGluke."

"Tonight?"

"Whenever. I suppose tonight's best."

"Sure, I will, but I don't know—"

"Unlikely suspect, you're thinking, but everybody's unlikely until someone isn't. What does he do at Breedtown? Who does he see?"

"Want me to question him? Bring him in?"

Charleston gave me his slow smile. "Not yet, Jase. Not yet if ever. Question a half-wit, and you get half-witted answers."

He put on his silver-gray hat and left me to the typewriter.

I was finished before noon, and the long day lay ahead of me. I joshed with Jimmy Conner for a while and went out on the street and saw Amussen in the police car, making sure that law and order prevailed. It was prevailing, all right, and would have been without him.

Yesterday's wind had spent itself, after wrenching some limbs from the trees that decorated the courthouse lawn and rolling milkshake containers in the gutters. The town wasn't very keen on tidiness, but the sky was tidy, not a tatter of cloud in it, and the sun was asking things to grow, fast, before frost. I wondered what happened to wind. Leaving us, did it sweep east to torment far neighbors? It was hard to think it just lay down and played dead.

I shied away from the Commercial Cafe and Jessie Lou and walked to Hamm's Big Hamburger for lunch. The burger was big enough but, as always, was layered in a store-bought roll that only famine could relish. No wonder kids went for ketchup. I washed the thing down and promised my stomach something better for dinner.

Afterwards I lounged up and down Main Street without seeing Luke. The town seemed ready for the last rites. I poked my head in the Bar Star. It had everything necessary for a saloon except customers. Mike Day came out of his bank, looking prosperous, and patted one of his setters. "Hot on the trail of the murderer, I suppose," he said to me.

"Still sniffing around. Any bloodhound strain in your dogs?"

He ignored the question as not worthy of notice. He smiled while taking a deep breath, as if the atmosphere of the bank dulled him even though it was spiked with ten-percent interest. "I do believe I can help you. How would your office like a Ouija board as a gift? I think I can get my board of directors to approve. Or maybe we could engage a good fortuneteller." He didn't mean to sting me, I realized. He just liked his own sense of humor.

"Thanks," I said, "but wait till we ask a few more questions." I added as a comeback, "You're next on the list." I didn't know how close to right I was.

"It would be easy to think you're dumb, Jase," he answered, not to be offensive. "Just a dumb kid that a star happened to fall on his shirt. Questions? Come on with them. Come one and all. Hear the big banker sing."

"What's the tune?"

"Washed in the blood of the lamb, meaning ignorance of any wrongdoing, meaning innocence, total."

"Lily white?" I said.

"As the driven snow." He walked away, chest out, in the direction of the post office, his two setters following. He did own the bank.

It had come about time to go home for supper. I lazed along on the way there and remembered of a sudden that I hadn't called the office all day. I stopped at our one and only outside telephone booth. Jimmy Conner said Charleston had driven out to his place and didn't expect to be back that night, barring emergencies. Nothing doing at the office to upset anyone's bowels except that Amussen, the damn Swede or whatever, hadn't come to relieve him, being too busy in his lofty job as town marshal. So would I stop and get grub for the jail's one customer?

I trailed off to the Commercial Cafe and got it. Jessie Lou was too busy to cast more than a glance at me, which was all that I wanted.

I delivered the meal and went home and had supper and stuck around for a time, thinking things downtown wouldn't pick up for an hour or more. I helped Mother with the dishes, had a bath and looked in on my father, who had his nose in a book as per custom. Then I took off.

At the Bar Star, to me the most likely place, a four-handed poker game was just getting started at a table that had seen plenty of action in its time. I knew the players, well or barely. One was Ward Yonce, a big wheat-grower in the east end of the county. One was Sylvester Black, a relative newcomer who owned the Chevrolet agency. The others were Felix Underwood and Frank Featherston, both good credit risks. That crowd didn't play penny ante. I spoke to them while the chips were being counted out. They knew better than to think I was about to put a crimp in their game. No one ever had.

In one of the low-backed booths, close by, Chuck Cleaver sat. A medium-sized stockgrower, he was known to go on a joyous bust once in a while. Right now he was pouring himself a drink from a half-empty bottle. His attention went from it to an electrified cattle prod, or goad, angled at his side. It was one of those things, battery-operated, with a push button fixed to the handle. Activated and in contact with target, they delivered jolt enough to put the run on the meanest of cows. Once I had seen a horse touched with a prod. It produced a startled explosion of wind that shot the horse over a fence. Cleaver's possession looked new. It might be the first he ever owned.

I bought a bottle of beer from Bob Studebaker and sat in a booth next to Cleaver's. I doubted he saw me, he was that absorbed.

The place was hot, holding close the memory of the afternoon sun. It was still, too, and filling up with smoke. I took off my jacket and sipped at my beer, asking myself if McGluke would show up at all. He hadn't by the time I emptied the bottle.

I got up and went to the bar for another beer I didn't want. "Hot," I said to Studebaker.

"Who says any different?"

"Luke McGluke been around?"

"Earlier." Studebaker rested his forearms on the bar. "Funny question. What do you want that goony guy for?"

"Who said I wanted him?"

"You just did."

"All right. I'm making a study. Abnormal psychology."

"College boy," Studebaker said as if the words explained everything. "Abnormal psychology, now that's a wide field. When I have time, I'll make out a list of my customers. Always ready to aid education, I am."

"Thanks. You expect McGluke to come back?"

"Sooner or later. He's got to swamp out." He turned away and began rinsing glasses. From the table behind me someone called, "Another round, Bob."

I went back toward my booth with my beer. The poker game was heating up, though you wouldn't know it without knowing the players. They sat quiet, smoking and drinking, their whole attention on the cards and on one another, as if the flick of an eye or the turn of a mouth might be revealing. Ward Yonce and Sylvester Black were winning. Felix Underwood fingered what was left of his chips. Barring a turn in his luck, Frank Featherston would have to buy soon.

In his booth Chuck Cleaver sang to himself. I guessed the tune was "Red Wing," old theme song of the bunkhouse. He grinned at me while he sang. I took my seat.

I had just settled myself when McGluke entered. From the doorway he looked around, wary as an antelope. Sensing no danger, he walked past me. I had time to notice he was dressed right for the heat, in a tattered shirt and a pair of jeans worn thin at the seat.

He was about to edge past the poker players when Chuck Cleaver saw him. A sudden smile of inspiration split Cleaver's face. I should have known what was coming. At the right instant Cleaver touched Luke's threadbare behind with the prod and pushed the button.

From almost a standstill McGluke leaped to the top of the poker table. The table collapsed, spilling McGluke and the chips. Three chairs went over, their occupants with them. Only Featherston still had a seat, and one of McGluke's thrashing legs brought him down. Over the clatter a voice sounded. "What the Jesus Christ hell!"

From the bar Studebaker yelled, "For God's sake cut it out."

Ward Yonce reared up on his hands and sang out, "Quit swinging at me." It was a chair leg that had hit him. He reached out a hand to rake in some chips and got hit again.

Luke McGluke got to a half-crouch and tried to back out, again presenting his butt to Chuck Cleaver. Cleaver calculated, his tongue poked out at the side of his mouth, found the right spot and pushed the button again.

The curtain rose for an encore.

Studebaker ran from behind the bar. I jumped up and grabbed the prod from Cleaver. "That's enough."

"Just touched him up a little. Gimme my prod back."

"Not yet."

The scramble came untangled. McGluke ran for the rear. At the back door he shied one look over his shoulder. I was standing there with the prod.

"That crazy bastard!" Black said to Studebaker. "What

goosed him?" He looked at me, holding the prod. "You?"

"Not me," I answered.

Studebaker didn't like fights. He said, "I guess he just got a wild hair."

"The goddamn chips," Yonce said, picking up some. He straightened up. "Someone's going to pay for this, by Jesus!"

It was then that Felix Underwood started laughing, not giggling, not chuckling, but laughing from deep in the belly. I didn't know an undertaker could get tickled so.

By and by they were all grinning. Studebaker pushed up another table. I gave the prod back to Chuck Cleaver. He danced out, delighted.

Then I went through the back door to the lean-to where Luke McGluke slept. I wanted to tell him I wasn't guilty, but he wouldn't answer my knock and his door was locked.

I figured he had retired for the night, and I went on home. Not until I was on the way there did I start laughing myself.

Chapter
Ten

AFTER I HAD TOLD Charleston about Luke McGluke and the poker game the next morning and he had quit laughing, he said, "You have to tell Jimmy and Halvor. There's not fun enough in our work."

His smile faded slowly. "All the same, it was a mean thing to do, using that cattle prod on McGluke. You ever been on the receiving end of one of those things?"

I said I hadn't and never wanted to be.

He looked at the window, not as if to see anything through it. "Mostly what's funny isn't so funny on second thought." He might have been talking to himself. "Except for nonsense, humor is based on pathos or hurt. Ever read 'Stay Away Joe'?"

"No."

"Funniest damn story you maybe ever will read, but underneath it's sad. It's pathetic."

It wasn't often Charleston let such reflections speak out, and for a moment I didn't break into his thoughts, thinking he might say more, while I wondered whether he wasn't delaying the business at hand.

Then I said, "Never laugh, huh?"

"Oh, hell, laugh. Laugh yourself sick. There's little enough to laugh about. Later you can look underneath."

His gaze moved from the window and came to me. "Nothing last night to put on the record."

"Except for my own amusement, I guess."

He hitched forward in his chair. "I haven't told you. Becker's gone to work for Chuck Cleaver. He came to me, full of sweet innocence, and asked if he could. Well, sure. He's still in the county, in easy reach.

"Could I ask if you got anything more out of him?"

"Not one thing." He sighed. "I'm still looking for a pry."

I waited, wanting him to give me my day's instructions.

He went on, "Meantime we're stuck on dead center. Suspects? Sure, plenty of them, but where's the evidence? Becker knows something, but we don't know what. Then there's Old Woman Gray Wolf, unlikely but possible. There's Eagle Charlie and Rosa and Red Fall, the true believer. No more than fringe people so far as we know. Count your nutcake, Luke McGluke, for what he's worth."

"My guess is not much," I said.

"Take in all Breedtown," he went on as if he hadn't heard me. "Take in everyone who didn't like Grimsley. That's a damn army."

"You want to pick one for me?" I asked.

Again he paid no attention. "The county commissioners meet today. I'm meeting with them. We need more money, Jase."

I agreed without saying so.

"None of you make enough," he continued. "I can squeeze out a poor salary for another deputy, but not if I pay the present staff what they're worth." The flat of his hand hit the desk. "That damn marshal's job I got saddled with! Mostly it's wasted money, but who'd be the first to yell if Halvor isn't seen cruising the town?"

"The county commissioners."

"And the mayor and the school people and all. And here we are with a murder on our hands. Pisswillie."

He still hadn't told me what to do, but now, as if reading my thoughts, he said, "There's some papers you can serve. Civil proceedings."

"All right."

"Then relieve Jimmy for a while. He ought to let the wind blow him."

I answered, "He gets stubborn."

"I'll speak to him."

"No McGluke?" I asked.

"What do you think?"

"I don't think anything. Last night sure didn't give me a clue."

"There's maybe nothing there. Probably isn't, but—"

"I get you. Leave no stone unturned."

His big smile, missing for some time, came to his face. He wasn't a man to let troubles down him for very long. "Good boy," he said. "We'll make out, Jase."

By noon I had served the papers he'd given me. Then I went home and had lunch, milk and a sandwich not made of those chemical rolls, and bought grub for Jimmy's one customer and tried to get Jimmy out of the office.

"What's the idea," he said, "the sheriff and you both wantin' me gone?"

I told him he worked too long and too hard.

"So what do I do?" he asked. "Play cards, get drunk, manhandle some bastard, go to a whorehouse of which there ain't any? All of a sudden why worry about me?"

"The sheriff wants you to keep in tiptop shape. Get some fresh air. Breathe deep. Exercise."

He said, "Oh, shit," and looked down at his splayed feet, shod in cracked gaiters. One of the gaiters had been cut to allow for a bunion. "Why don't you tell me to take a long walk?"

"Three blocks isn't so long. You can make it to the Club Pool Hall and play gin."

"Happy day," he said and creaked up from his chair and creaked out after getting his hat.

Time dragged by. Amussen checked in by phone. There were a couple of other calls, neither important. Charleston dodged in, got a nothing-doing shake of my head and left with some papers he took from his desk.

At four o'clock Amussen phoned again, on schedule. He asked, "Anything for me, Hawkshaw?"

"Duke Appleby has locked himself out of his car and can't get help. Mechanics all busy. But maybe he's rolling by now."

"I'll run by."

"The dogs are howling again."

"Old Mrs. Godsby, huh?"

"Good guess."

"Invisible dogs, howls not howled. The poor, damned old soul. I'll go by and tell her I put the run on the pack."

He hung up and left me thinking about age and hallucinations and dogs barking from the fringes of death. He left me thinking about himself, too. Smart he wasn't, kind he was.

An hour later Jimmy came in, smelling of pool-hall smoke. "For one goddamn dollar," he said, "I walk six blocks and play a thousand hands, allow one or two either way. Get out from the phone, kid."

"Big winner. What else is exciting?"

"Nothing, except I helped the tomfool start his barrel of bolts. Battery corroded, that was all. No contact."

I asked, "What tomfool, Jimmy?"

"What do you think, we're all nuts? You wouldn't be so far off the mark at that. Luke McGluke, that's who."

"Where was he headed?"

"I didn't ask, and he didn't say. He started down the street, prayin' to get somewhere, I guess."

"South?"

"Down the street is south."

I said, "Thanks." South was in the direction of Breedtown.

As I was about to take off, Charleston came in. "All day," he said. "All the damn day. Fiddle and faddle, and we'll get to you soon, Mr. Sheriff. And then the time comes and they say we have to think about the taxpayers, and they're not very happy, not with a murderer loose and no progress to date."

He was speaking as he moved to his inner office. I followed him. "And you know what they'd say if we solved the case quick? Sure. Why try to improve on perfection?"

He sat down in his chair and grinned and with his hand asked me to be seated. "Just spouting off, Jase," he said. "We won out, though. Now quit your bitching. Hear me, you there?"

"Plain as day," I answered. "Now could I ask a nonbitchy question?"

"Not unless you have to."

"Yes, sir. Luke McGluke is out in his car, bound for Breedtown like as not."

"Uh-huh!" he said. "But that's not a question."

"Here it is. Do I follow him now or later?"

He took time to think, then answered, "What could you get in daylight? What at night for that matter? Just who he sees, maybe. A piece of conversation, which is even more maybe. The odds say it's a wild-goose chase, but when there's nothing else to chase, what do you chase but the goose?"

There was only one answer to that, and I didn't say it.

"Make it under cover of night," he said.

In the month of June darkness holds off until ten o'clock and even later, so I didn't set out for Breedtown until twilight was dying. I drove the unmarked office car.

Before I reached there, the sky had turned black. I felt enveloped in the close dark, with nothing to guide me but the twin tunnels my headlights bored. It would be easy, I thought, for a man to lose himself, to surrender himself to the blind world. Just turn out the lights and leave the car and be absorbed in the unseeing universe, breathing its breath, heart beating to its slow beat. Be a forever-night wanderer, lost and free.

Enough of tomfoolery on a tomfool's trail.

Now what to do when I arrived? I could hardly break in on a social gathering. And if I did, what would I get? Only the knowledge that McGluke was in so-and-so's shack, where it was his right to be, all men being equal. I could only sneak close and watch and listen, hoping for a betraying action or word.

I parked the car short of the turn-in and stumbled on in the dark. Somewhere ahead was a two-plank footbridge across the creek. A limb stung my cheek. I had blundered into a bush. I caught my toe on a stick and stooped and picked it up. It would do for a cane to poke ahead with and so make sure of my footing. I found the bridge.

The scattered glow of kerosene lamps began to help me. I counted six. Two came from the little cluster of buildings that housed Eagle Charlie and with him, I supposed, Rosa and the old squaw. One shone from the shack where Pambrun and Framboise lived. The others I couldn't account for.

I could see now that some automobiles sagged close to the buildings, like worn-out horses. By squinting I could identify Luke McGluke's car. It was parked some distance away, at a turn in the lane, which wasn't a lane at all but only a trail worn by wheels. If Eagle Charlie's machine was there, I couldn't see it.

Of a sudden dogs began barking. I planked myself flat on the ground. I had been a fool not to think about dogs. I lay quiet, cursing under my breath, expecting them to charge out. When they didn't, I wet a finger and tested the wind. Whatever breeze seemed to blow seemed to blow my way. Then, ignored and unnoticed before, the bark-cry of a coyote sounded from somewhere out in the hills. The dogs barked back. I wouldn't be smelled out at least.

I went ahead, crouching, feeling ahead with my stick, though the light had grown better. I lay down at the edge of the lane, thinking to crawl closer if need be. Voices muted by walls came to my ears. I couldn't make out any words. Ground chill and night chill began penetrating my clothes. The coyote called again, and the dogs answered. For minutes I stayed where I was, debating what next to do, wondering just where to go if I crawled closer. It was while I figured that the damn moon sailed free of clouds and shone silver and bright on all the land. Away and away I could see the sharp lift of the mountains. ⟨

A door opened, letting out the walled voices, and the figure of Luke McGluke outlined itself in the doorway. The door closed, corralling the voices, and McGluke started moving away.

I did a stupid thing then. I did two stupid things.

I came to my feet and called out, "McGluke!"

His head turned my way, his eyes shining with moonlight. He stood for one instant, then started to run. I threw down my stick and took out after him.

I could run faster in spite of his stride. Like many big men, he was awkward and slow. His feet didn't track. To the thud of our steps the dogs began clamoring. I tackled McGluke just short of his car. We both went down. A wailing cry came out of him, like the keening of a nanny jackrabbit I once shot in the guts.

It was like fighting a rail-and-wire fence—all posts, poles and spikes and stringy line. Master one, and another tormented you. Dogs circled us, yapping. One nipped my leg.

Just as I thought I'd brought him under control, I lost my senses in one quick dazzle of light.

"He's coming around," a voice said.

"Take him a while," another said. "That's one hell of a knot on his head."

My hand come up, not that I'd ordered it to. It felt a damp cloth and moved it off my eyes and head. My eyes saw a plank ceiling. It moved in on me and drew back.

"Easy, man," the second voice said. "Don't rush it." The cloth, gently replaced, closed me off again.

The voices came clearer. There were at least three of them. One asked, "Why was he chasing McGluke?"

"Only he knows."

"Sorry he did, I bet, when he comes to."

"Double sorry that McGluke found that rock."

I heard myself say, "Take it off, please."

A careful hand lifted it. The back of the hand was haired out and the bare forearm furred, both with red. The gentle hand put the cloth aside.

"Feeling better now?" The speaker was Red Fall. I moved my head and saw Framboise and Pambrun on either side of him. I realized then I was in their shack.

"Beginning to," I answered. I managed to sit up. All eyes had questions in them. I didn't answer, saying instead, "Fool business. If McGluke hadn't run—"

Framboise said, "He was scared."

"He's always scared," Pambrun added.

"Poor man." Fall shook his head sadly. I wondered if he were troubled by the thought that God had failed man in one case at least. Or played a joke on him. "We can hope he didn't wreck that old car of his."

"He took off like crazy," Pambrun said.

"We didn't think to hold him," Framboise told me, and again all eyes were asking questions.

"You heard us, I guess?" I said.

"Heard you and the dogs and, oh, man, that—what you call it?—that blat, that wail of his," Framboise answered.

"It doesn't matter," I told them. "My car's down the road. I'm going home."

They doubted that I was ready, but I made for the door. Pambrun and Framboise went along with me, making sure I got to the car.

I did and drove home with an ache in my head.

Chapter Eleven

I GOT UP EARLY to the ring of the alarm clock I had set. My father and mother would learn soon enough that I had been hit on the head. Why agitate them at breakfast and have to argue that the life of a deputy was not really dangerous in spite of appearances?

The mirror told me that the broken bruise on my head had seeped some blood during the night. The swelling had gone down, though, in proportion, it looked like, to the spread from it of black, blue and sickly yellow. I washed the blood off, shaved, used some talcum powder, dressed and went out, being careful to close the door quietly. For comfort I had to wear my hat at a considerable angle. Jaunty wasn't word enough for it.

A few early birds were feeding at the Commercial Cafe. Their morning gloom kept them from noticing me, blue being blue, inside or out. Jessie Lou wasn't on shift. The fry cook, a new man and fat, asked me what I'd have. He saw my bruise but said nothing, in the manner of one accustomed to carnage. I ordered a short stack and coffee. The pancakes were light and lightened my spirits.

I whiled away a half-hour or so on the street while the town came to life. At a little before eight o'clock I entered the office.

Jimmy lifted his eyes from the telephone, saw me and

said, "Jumpin' Jesus! Hold on. I'll find a Purple Heart. Or
was it a door you ran into like everyone else?"

"Mine was different," I answered. "It was rock."

"What in hell happened? You ain't fit for duty."

"I'm fit, Jimmy, but let the rest lie for a while. I made
a fool of myself and feel extra delicate."

"Seen Doc Yak, Jase?"

"No need to. I'm curing up."

The outer door opened, letting in Charleston. His face
sobered into questions when he saw me. He didn't speak
them. He just motioned me into the inner office. The first
thing he asked was not what had happened, as might
be expected from another man, but "Are you all right,
Jase?"

"I'm sure. Don't go by my looks."

We sat down, and I told him about last night, omitting
nothing that I remembered. He nodded a couple of times
while I talked. "A damn sorry thing," he said, his eyes
sympathetic as they re-examined the bruise. "Glad it
wasn't more serious, though. It might have killed
you." His gaze met mine. "The question is: Why did
McGluke run from you? What's he got to hide? I aim
to find out."

"I don't know how important that is," I said. "He spooks
easy. What's first in my mind is those red hairs on Fall's
hands and arms. You ought to have a look. They're thick,
and they're long."

"All in time, Jase," he answered as if brushing the subject aside. "All in good time. Now we have to have a talk
with McGluke. You didn't happen to see him this morning?"

"He's probably still asleep in that lean-to back of the
Bar Star."

"I'll rout him out." The trace of a smile came on his mouth. "I doubt you're the proper man for it." He moved as if to go.

"Neither are you," I said, feeling a little stung though common sense told me he hadn't meant to sting. "I'm sorry, but I would send Jimmy."

"Send Jimmy?"

"Yes, sir. There's a reason. Yesterday Jimmy helped McGluke start his old car. How many men would have done that? McGluke will remember. What's more, Jimmy has a way about him when he wants to use it."

"We'll try it." Charleston called out, "Hey, Jimmy."

Jimmy poked his head in the door and followed it inside as he spoke. "That's my name."

"Jase, here, has a job for you."

With his eyes turned to me Jimmy asked, "He the high sheriff all of a sudden?"

"Don't bristle, Jimmy. You know I always take good advice, from you or anyone else. Jase says it's a job only you can do. I'm with him."

"Well, now," Jimmy said, "if you put it that way—"

"We want to talk to Luke McGluke. Jase believes if any man can bring him in without a fight or a chase, that man's you. What about it?"

"I can sure as hell try." Jimmy was smiling now. "No rough stuff. Gentle is the ticket, kind of soothing, you might say."

"Soothe him in. Jase will take any calls. Fix the jack, will you?"

We didn't have a switchboard, though we called it a board, but three phones and a jack on Jimmy's desk that was used to switch calls.

Jimmy left, and Charleston began fingering slips on his desk. "I wonder if I have time to go to the bank."

For an instant he was quiet. He lifted his head and studied a bare wall, his hands still. "The bank," he said. "Yeah, the bank. Jase, when all else fails, visit your friendly banker."

The phone rang, and I answered it. Halvor was checking in. I had hardly hung up when it rang again. On the line was the deputy sheriff stationed at Petroleum. He wanted to talk to Charleston. They talked for quite a while, though I doubted that Charleston paid full attention. He wore an absent-minded smile during the conversation and kept tapping with a pencil. At any rate nothing urgent appeared to have come up.

We barely heard the outer door open. Not until the inner one swung could we make out words. Jimmy was saying, "Just be calm there, Luke. There's nothing to be afraid of. I swear to that. Take my word. I'm your friend, boy."

He entered with McGluke while still talking. "Mr. Sheriff," he went on, "I'm here to see that nobody hurts Mr. McGluke."

McGluke's eyes were scared. His Adam's apple bobbed as if to words he couldn't say.

Charleston said, "Why, come in, Luke. Take a chair. No harm in us. Be easy."

McGluke was letting Jimmy steer him toward a chair when he caught sight of me. A shout that was half scream came from him. His long arm reached out, and a long, shaky finger pointed at me. "No! Not him! Not him! He's bad. He's bad to me."

He wheeled around to run and collided with Jimmy.

For his age Jimmy was strong. His hands closed on McGluke's arms. "Hold it, Luke. Hold it, boy. We won't let him hurt you. If he's bad to you, we'll make it damn bad for him. There, now."

Charleston added, "Whoa, Luke. We promised no one would hurt you. No one will."

McGluke allowed Jimmy to turn him back, facing inside. In spite of the assurances he looked as terrified as a bronc under first saddle. He pointed that shaky finger at me again. "It was him. A joke, maybe, he thinks."

Charleston swung in his chair so as to face me. His voice was loud and rough with accusation. "What's this all about, Mr. Beard? Tell us! I want the truth. You heard Mr. McGluke."

McGluke couldn't wait for me to speak. His voice was still high. "No lie. He has a lightning stick. He pokes me with it. It jumps you. Oh, by God, anyone jumps."

"Where did he poke you?" Charleston asked.

"In the ass. I shit almost."

Charleston put a hand over his mouth. "I didn't mean that. I mean where were you?"

"In the saloon, and last night he wants to poke me again."

Two and two came together in my mind and made a neat four. McGluke had seen me in the Bar Star, holding the cattle prod I had taken from Chuck Cleaver. And last night, when I called to him, I had in my hand a length of tree limb that I used as a cane. In the moonlight it could have been taken for an electrified goad.

"You got me wrong, Luke," I said. "It's all a mistake."

I explained then while they listened. McGluke, if he understood, still appeared less than satisfied. His Adam's apple kept bobbing.

"So you can see it wasn't Mr. Beard," Charleston said after I'd finished. "He wouldn't torment you. Natural mistake, but he wouldn't. Now that that's settled, Luke, let's see if you can help us. That's why you're here, to help if you can. Please tell me. You go to Breedtown pretty often. What do you do there?"

"Visit, sit, maybe eat. They treat me good. That's all."

"Better than you get treated in town?"

"Sure. Better. Real good."

"I understand. Now we're trying to find out who killed F. Y. Grimsley. You've heard about that."

The phone rang, and Jimmy, in order not to interrupt, went to the outer office to answer, saying as he left, "Just call out if you need me, Luke."

McGluke said, "He was a no-good man, that Grimsley." He looked in the direction Jimmy had gone as if to assure himself a friend was in reach. "He was bad to me."

"Someone was bad to him, too, bad enough to kill him. Did you get any ideas from the talk at Breedtown, any ideas about who knocked him in the head?"

"Talk is all. Nobody felt sorry. Oh, maybe Eagle Charlie a little."

"You didn't pick up anything that would help us? Nothing from Eagle Charlie, Rosa, Mrs. Gray Wolf, Red Fall, anybody?"

"Nobody. They're all right. Red Fall, too."

"What made you mention him, Luke? Why pick him out?"

"He doesn't live there. He comes, and he goes, just like me. He talks to the old woman."

"Through Rosa?"

"Sure. Different talk, you know."

"And that's all you know?"

"About Breedtown, that's all."

Charleston leaned forward and rested his forearms on the desk. "If you hear anything, will you let us know? All right, and thanks, Luke. You can go now."

After he'd gone, Jimmy came back into the room.

"One thing's explained," Charleston told us. "At Breedtown they treat him like a human being, maybe more so. The Indians have a special attitude, a sort of kind and hands-off attitude toward people not right in the head."

"Not like in town," Jimmy put in. "Bunch of jokers around here."

"Make it sons of bitches, Jimmy. Unthinking but cruel sons of bitches." Charleston got to his feet. "All right. To the bank. Better bring your pad, Jase."

But we didn't get to see Mike Day until late afternoon. The cashier, name of Keith Morris, who looked as if figures were his dish for breakfast, lunch and supper, said Day was appraising some property. He had left word he'd be back, though.

Charleston spent the time going over papers, dictating to Jody Lester, his part-time stenographer, and talking to Rod Smith, the newspaper editor, who was maybe as good a newshound as I was a detective. I relieved Jimmy again.

The bank was closed to customers when we knocked on the door. The setters had moved aside to let us approach. Morris undid the lock, saying as we went in, "Mr. Day is in his office." His head inclined toward a back room where Day did his thinking.

Day rose from his chair and shook hands. His left hand held a cigar. "Mighty good to see you," he said, blowing smoke through his hail-fellow smile. Then, "Good Lord, Jase, get socked with a ball bat or what?"

"A pebble," I said.

"Well, have a chair, you two. I bet they've kept you boys on the jump, what with a murder and all."

"That's what we're here for, to see where to land if we can," Charleston said.

"Why, sure. Of course. It's here for you, any assistance we can give you, any help within reason. I'm mighty puzzled, though, mighty puzzled you should come here, but you can bet your bottom dollar on us." He puffed out a plume of puzzled smoke.

"That's good," Charleston said, taking on the smile that Day had lost. "I was afraid you might be a little standoffish."

"Standoffish?" Day let the word roll around in his head. "Discreet, yes. Standoffish, no. But you must realize there are matters we must consider private affairs."

"Like bank statements? Like deposits?"

"In specific cases I'm afraid so. You understand that a bank stands in a confidential relationship with its clients. It's privileged information, like a doctor's or lawyer's. We mustn't betray our trust."

I wanted to answer "Bullshit." Day had skated on the thin edge of the law until a lucky break made him respectable. That much I knew.

Charleston asked, "Dave Becker banks with you, doesn't he?"

"Obviously you know that much. It's not a secret. So yes, he does. He's a valued client. Good balance always. No overdrafts."

"I want the dope on him for the last year or two. Show me the records."

Day put his cigar in a tray with thoughtful attention to

it. "I must say no," he said to the cigar. "No, unless you have his consent. You can appreciate my position."

Charleston wasn't smiling anymore. "It's murder, and to hell with you, Mike, and to hell with your pretty scruples. So answer up and answer all right."

"I really can't, Chick. The confidential relationship remains."

Charleston got up abruptly. "Keep those records intact. I'm going for a subpoena."

Day rammed his chair back. "My God, Chick, you can't do that! Subpoena the statements! Think of the good name of the bank, man."

Charleston said, "Too bad. Too bad the bank obstructs justice. Come on, Jase."

Day moved from behind his desk and came forward, his hands out. "Don't leave, Chick. Don't leave in a huff. You've upset me. I haven't had time to think."

"The records," Charleston said.

A big, tired sigh came out of Day, leaving him slumped. He trudged to the door, opened it and called, "Keith." After he'd received a "Yes, sir," he went on, "Dig out the stuff on Dave Becker for the last couple of years. Bring it in, please." He went back to his chair, sank in it and said, "You've forced me to compromise my principles."

"First time for everything," Charleston answered.

After a minute Morris came in with pages of figures and put them on Day's desk, his face one sad cipher. He went out.

"Use my desk," Day said, rising.

"All right. May want to question you."

"I'll be in front."

"Right now," Charleston told me as he fingered papers,

"Dave Becker has seven thousand plus in the bank. Pretty hefty, huh?"

"Unless he saved every nickel," I said.

Charleston was too busy to hear me. Maybe ten minutes passed. Then he said, "Get Day back here, Jase."

After I did, he asked Day, "Mike, didn't these deposits strike you as strange?"

Day had seated himself in a chair not his own, since Charleston occupied his. He said, "I don't pay close attention. He kept a nice balance. That's what I know and no more."

"He earned a hundred dollars a month. He banked that pay pretty regularly, within a week after he got it. But, now, here and there and numerous places, he deposited a hundred, two hundred, one hundred and fifty and, right here, is five hundred. No regularity about those. All in cash, if I read right. Cash." His eyes bored at Day.

"I don't know," Day said. "How would I know?"

"I don't think you did. I don't think anyone paid much attention. A man can make quite a little stake in a poker game, no questions asked."

Day said, "He didn't gamble. Not Becker, I'm sure."

"So am I. Put these in a safe place and seal up what you know. Thanks, Mike."

Charleston and I went out, leaving Day looking at his ashtray.

Outside, Charleston told me, "We found our pry, Jase, but night's about here and we've worked long enough. We'll use it tomorrow."

We didn't, though. There were other developments.

Chapter
Twelve

JIMMY CONNER'S VOICE screeched through the closed door. "Goddamn it! Where is everybody? Goddamn it!"

I opened the door to the repeated click of the telephone receiver. The time was eight o'clock, lacking ten minutes.

Jimmy looked up from the desk. Pambrun and Framboise stood near him, their hats in their hands. "Thank God for small favors," Jimmy said, replacing the phone.

I asked, "What's the matter?"

"Matter, goddamn it! Plenty the matter. Another man dead, that's what's the matter, and no one but me here. No son of a bitch answers phones. Where's Charleston?"

"Who's dead?"

"Eagle Charlie, that's who."

I said, "Eagle Charlie?" not believing.

The two breeds nodded as I turned to them. Pambrun spoke one word. "Killed."

Jimmy asked again, "Where in hell's Charleston?" His eyes flicked to the big clock on the wall as if to hurry it. It didn't read quite eight o'clock yet.

"Driving in," I answered. "What you expect?"

Jimmy wouldn't shut up. "I been ringin' him regular. You, too, and Halvor. No one home, no one comin' in. Just me here. Shit!" He flung out his hands. "Tiptop outfit, this is, modern, like smoke signals."

He had right on his side. We weren't advanced enough for communication between office and car, the commissioners being careful of taxpayers' money. I said, "Ease off. He'll be here."

I had never seen Jimmy rattled before. Age, I thought, and for an instant reflected that age rattled all of us. "Mind if we go into the other office?" I asked.

"I don't mind a damn thing."

"Give me an outside line then."

We went in, Pambrun, Framboise and I. They had kept silent while Jimmy spouted. It struck me as we seated ourselves that Jimmy might be relieved to have had the buck pass.

"All right," I said. "He's dead. You sure?"

"I seen dead men before," Pambrun replied.

"We found him," Framboise said.

"Where? How? All of it, please."

"Outside, close to his own door. Maybe six—eight steps away." Pambrun's gaze met that of Framboise in the silent communication I had noticed before. "Hit on the head."

Framboise corrected him, a note of apology in his voice. "Knocked is better, Pete. Knocked in the head. Knocked in the head dead. A little blood but not much. Skull bone broke, I think."

"And you two found him? Before anyone else?"

"First up, you know. All the time, pret' near, we are first out of bed. So we found him dead. We told Rosa. We got a blanket and covered him." Pambrun had spoken as if in conclusion, but Framboise added, "Then, right away, we drove here."

I had taken notes. "The sheriff's due any minute," I told them. "Now hold on." I lifted the phone and called outside, to Doc Yak first, then Felix Underwood. Both were startled. Doc Yak was grumpy.

As I hung up, Charleston came in. He didn't say hello. He said to me, "Got the dope?"

"Enough for now, I guess."

"Eagle Charlie. For a fact?" The breeds' heads gave him the answer. "Who in hell—?" The heads didn't know.

Charleston asked a couple of brisk questions, to which I already had answers. He told me, "Notify Doc Yak and Felix."

"I just did. They'll be starting out any minute."

"All right. Come on, all of you." He led the way outside to his Special. In passing, I noticed the car that Pambrun and Framboise must have driven in. It might have been the first number off the line when Ford began building V-8s.

Charleston drove with silent and steady purpose, almost as if the mere turn of the wheels were an end in itself. Not once during the trip did he open his mouth. Trouble, I thought, was a good silencer, even if uncommon with him. We didn't speak, either. He turned off the highway and tooled up the side road, splashing water at the creek crossing.

A couple of dozen people, probably the whole population of Breedtown except cradled babies, stood around a blanketed shape, their eyes going from it to us and back again. The noise of our engine died. In its stead came high wailings from inside a cabin. The dogs slunk around. Not a one barked.

"All right," Charleston said, getting out. "Get back, you people!" They didn't go far.

Underwood wheeled up in his ambulance and said as he

hit the ground, "I can't believe it. Not Eagle Charlie."

No one answered. Charleston was bending down. He moved the blanket off the head and glanced up at Underwood as if to say "See for yourself."

Peering, Underwood said, "By God if it ain't."

"Doc Yak's on the way," Charleston told him as if that item provided enough information for now. His hand was exploring the thick mat of gray hair. There was some blood in it, dried. I saw his hand feel and his eyes look and saw his hand come away and saw what his fingers held— a couple of red hairs. He slipped them into an envelope, saying nothing.

He stayed hunkered down a while longer, his hand exploring again. No one spoke. The high wailing, the keening of squaws bereaved, hurt my ears. For other sounds there was only the occasional, careful shuffling of feet.

We heard Doc Yak before we saw him approaching on foot, his satchel in his hand. He was proclaiming, "To hell with all crossings! To hell with infernal machines!" Looking beyond him, I could see his car was stuck in the ford, as mine had been.

"Who's the lucky man?" Doc Yak asked, coming up. At his best he wasn't much of a respecter of death. Fighting it day by day, he might have been affronted by it. "Eagle Charlie, huh? It saves the poor son of a bitch a whole lot of trouble."

The high wailing seemed to dispute him.

He stooped, unlatched his bag and got out his stethoscope. He bared the chest, listened, discarded the stethoscope and, as if it might be at fault, fingered for a pulse. "Routine," he said between his teeth. "They never get

any deader. Plain at first sight." Then, as if the keening
had just come to his ears, he burst out, "Tell them, for
Christ's sake, to shut up! Howling like coon dogs, but even
a damn hound knows a cold trail."

Charleston said quietly, "Calm down, Doc. You haven't
finished."

I looked away as Doc Yak examined the body. It wasn't
that I was afraid of corpses; they just made me want to
withdraw. The circle of watchers, broken to allow room
for official procedure, had spread into a straggling half-
circle. Through the gap I could see the upward slope of
the land, bright with the low-growing first blooms of the
season, with shades of purple, white and blue. Moss cam-
pion I recognized, and dwarf phlox and forget-me-nots.
Together they made what we called carpet flowers.

I turned my eyes to the intent, watching faces. They
tended to be high in the cheekbones. Some were dark,
some half-dark, some copper-tinted, some barely sugges-
tive of Indian blood. They were good faces, I thought,
good faces almost all, better than the circumstances of
their lives. Call them breeds, call them war-whoops, treat
them that way, and so put an end to hopes not ended
already.

Doc Yak stood up, through with his chore. He wiped his
hands on a cloth moistened by alcohol and passed it to
Charleston. "Skull cracked," he said, "and not just in one
place. That's what killed him."

Underwood, standing near, said, "The old blunt instrument again."

Doc turned on him like a terrier. "You and your fool
guesses! Blunt instruments don't bend. We told you that
once."

Unoffended, Underwood guessed again. "A blackjack, then. A leather poke filled with shot. It would bend."

"Given one hell of a swipe, maybe. Given a lot of arm."

"You think so?" Charleston asked. "Maybe the genuine article, Doc?"

"How in hell do I know? I didn't swing it."

"Dead how long, you estimate?"

"Questions," Doc replied. "All the time questions. Will he live, Doctor? Not likely, ma'am, seeing as he's already dead. Since when, Doctor? Ever since he met up with that old blunt instrument, maybe eight or ten or more hours ago. That's a guess." Doc closed his bag. "You can take him away, Felix."

To others of us Doc said with a smile that had some wolf in it, "Any pushers around? I need a fix."

"What you need," Underwood answered before he went for a stretcher, "is that morning coffee you missed. Better put a spike in it to boot."

I knew what Doc meant, though. With Doc at the wheel Pambrun and Framboise and I pushed his car out of the creek. I got my feet wet. Doc drove away without thanks.

After Eagle Charlie's body was put in the ambulance and the ambulance was rolling, Charleston drove us back to town, saying nothing until he parked in front of the Bar Star, then, "We'll lift one for old Eagle Charlie."

He pushed his way inside, holding the door for us. The one customer was Chuck Cleaver, who was working on a beer. To him Charleston said, "Your man in town?"

"Who?"

"Dave Becker."

"Nope."

"Where is he?"

"Helpin' truck a load of cattle, bound over the mountains. Left sometime early this morning."

"When's he due back?"

"Couple of days, something like that. Why, Sheriff?"

"How sure are you he'll come back? Tell me that."

Cleaver consulted his beer, thinking maybe it was better to look at than Charleston's face. "Pretty damn sure. I haven't paid him, for one thing."

Charleston asked, "What's another?"

"His job, but that ain't quite all. Just between us, Sheriff, I put him under bond, sort of. Only a fool lets his cows roll away without some protection. Right?"

"What kind of a bond?"

"It's kind of private, Sheriff, not everyone's business."

"Say it, anyhow."

"Him willin,' more or less, I put a lock on his bank account until he gets back. Now why all the questions?"

"Nothing. I just wanted to talk to him." Charleston shrugged and moved toward a table, saying to himself, "Pisswillie."

Tad Frazier came to the table to see what we'd have. He seemed a little surprised at the company Charleston and I kept. We had two rounds. Charleston paid for them and took us to the Commercial Cafe. Jessie Lou, waiting on us, gave me one slow gaze that seemed to say something, I didn't know what.

Afterwards, at the office, Charleston saw to the seating and said to Framboise and Pambrun, "You're not under suspicion, not by me, but there are a few questions I want to ask you."

The two men waited.

"Did you hear anything unusual last night?"

"Dogs barked, that was all," Pambrun answered. "Nothing. The damn dogs always bark."

"Did you have any visitors?"

Framboise took his turn. "Not that I seen, eh, Pete?"

"Not Luke McGluke? Not Red Fall, even?"

No, the men said with their heads.

"What about Dave Becker?"

I spoke out of turn. "He couldn't have been there, not according to Cleaver."

Charleston said, "You better think again, Jase. Cleaver says he left sometime early this morning. That leaves room." He went on, "No strange cars around?"

There hadn't been, he was told.

"Maybe you can straighten me out," Charleston said. "From what I hear, Eagle Charlie wasn't any great favorite, not with the women, anyhow. Mrs. Gray Wolf seemed to hate him. And yet they were crying over his death?"

Pambrun took time with his answer. "Eagle Charlie was a chief. All right, half-assed, but a chief. His father was a chief, and his father a chief honest to God. So we feel sorry. So women cry."

Framboise put in, "Indian women, they take time to be sad. Used to be they cut off their hair or maybe a finger. That was the old way. All the time crying out loud. So, today, they show sorry, too."

"All right," Charleston said. "Now tell me, what's in your minds? What strikes you? What questions?"

Pambrun answered, "The same one? Same man killed Grimsley and Eagle Charlie?"

"It looks like it. Someone, though, might have played copycat." When Framboise seemed not to understand, he explained, "Make-believe. Killed the same way. A second murderer, I mean. Make us believe he was the first. Yes, Framboise?"

"Grimsley, he blamed Breedtown. Yes?"

"For cattle rustling. Yes, pretty much."

"And the killings, they come home, too, home to Breedtown."

Framboise shifted in his chair. "Make-believe," he said. "Goddamn make-believe." It took me an instant to realize something had got under his skin. Realizing it, I could imagine that his eyes smoked and that a rise of blood made his dark face even darker. "Make-believe Breedtown, it's to blame. All the time blame damn Injun. Blame no-good breeds. White blood we got in us, most of us, but no. It's Injun blood bad."

Charleston held up his hand. "Whoa, now, Louis! I don't think that way. Neither does Jase. It might be someone at Breedtown. It might not. We have to start there, that's all. It's someone somewhere, and it's our job to find him whatever his blood. Got that?"

Pambrun's gaze went to Framboise, then to Charleston. He said, "Yes. We are sorry."

"All right. That's all, men. Thanks for your help."

On the way out, Framboise turned to me. "I didn't mean you," he said. "Pete and me sometime want to buy you a drink."

After they had gone, I said what I had been bursting to say. "Those red hairs! Two more. What do you make of them?"

"If we went to the state lab," Charleston told me, his speech and eyes thoughtful, "we'd have the state investigator on our necks."

It turned out we'd have him anyway, but now I said, "Why the state lab?"

"Jase, I can't tell. No equipment for it. But they might not be human hairs."

That night I dreamed about apes, great apes with long heels of hands that could crush a man's skull at a blow. They were all red and all hairy.

Chapter
Thirteen

"MR. JESUS is here," Halvor Amussen said, wagging his thumb toward the inner office. He stood by Jimmy's chair and had come in to report, I supposed, before setting out to ensure peace and quiet.

"Yeah," Jimmy chimed in. "The second coming has done come about."

They both grinned, waiting for me to catch on. I already had, or felt sure I had.

So, entering the inner office, I was prepared to see Cotton Mather, alias Inspector Gewald of the state attorney general's office. I had made his acquaintance two summers before and knew him to be a stern man with no sympathy for any offenders of the least letter of the law. At that time it had been our work, not his, that exposed a murderer.

He sat facing Charleston, his face somber and set. Charleston had just lighted his first cigar of the day. I knew it was the first because he didn't allow himself one until his workday began.

Charleston said, "You remember Inspector Gewald, Jase. He's here to help us."

Gewald shook my hand, not getting up. He had a no-nonsense grip. "How do you do, young man?"

I answered, all right, thinking I would be righter if he hadn't shown up.

"Glad you're here, Jase," Charleston said. "I was about to give Mr. Gewald a run-down on our crime wave."

"Just tell me what you can remember," Gewald asked. "I can see your written reports later." He eyed me. "I assume they're complete and up to date."

"They are."

Charleston settled himself in his chair, took a puff on the cigar and told the story.

When he was finished, Gewald asked, "That's all, is it?"

"My memory's pretty good."

It hadn't been, though. He had forgotten the red hairs. I interrupted, "But there's—"

Before I could say more, Charleston broke in. "Oh, yes. Perhaps I haven't emphasized sufficiently the hatred that old Mrs. Gray Wolf seemed to have for Eagle Charlie."

I knew enough then to shut up.

"I'm going to see those women," Gewald told Charleston. "I'll need your kid here."

"If you mean me," I said, "forget it."

Charleston hid with his hand what I hoped was a grin.

"Besides," I went on, "it wouldn't do any good. You can't get anything out of those women today. They're grieving. They're preparing for a funeral. It wouldn't be decent to break in on them now."

"Talkative," Gewald said to Charleston.

"When he needs to be."

"All right." Gewald got up. "We'll postpone that trip, waiting on the kid's sense of decency. I suppose you won't mind if I nose around some?"

"Nose all you want," Charleston replied. "Who am I to object?"

Gewald went out, not answering, his hat set straight and tight on his head.

It dodged into my mind as he closed the door that he was a solitary figure, a lonesome character, set as he was against all manner of human frailty. His rigidity set him apart from the common run, who needed some little margin for antics.

Charleston said, "You were about to let the cat out of the bag, eh, Jase?"

"About the red hairs, you mean? I thought you had forgotten."

"He'll find mention of them if he ever reads your reports. Meantime, let's keep our small secret."

"You've concluded the hairs are important, then?"

For a reason unknown to me, unless it was that he didn't want me too hot on a trail that might prove cold, he evaded my question. "What isn't important?"

I gave up on that subject. "What's on my plate today?"

"A break-in, for one thing. Roscoe Cromwell's summer cabin up on the Rose River. He usually moves there in July. Guy Jamison took a sashay by there and reported by telephone. Kids, probably, and long gone, but we have to investigate."

"Okay by me."

"Then this afternoon you can relieve Jimmy again, or Halvor, if he wants some time off. Their shifts are too long. You know that. Any idea for an addition to the force?"

"I've thought about Tad Frazier."

"Studebaker will howl his head off if we hire his bartender away, but sound Tad out, will you?"

"Yes, sir."

"While you work, I plan to vegetate." He opened a drawer and took out a book.

I asked, "Vegetate or cogitate?"

"College-man talk," he answered with his good smile. "I'm empty, and they say that reading maketh a full man." He let me see the title and author. I didn't pay much attention. The book was about cowboys, and the author's name was Ellison. I saw, too, the word "Mogollon."

"Back to the feud country, are you?" I said.

"Kind of. And one book leads to another."

"And to Dave Becker?"

"Who knows?" He leaned back and opened the book.

Through the outside door I saw rain was beginning to fall, so I took a slicker off its hook and threw it in the office car.

It turned out to be a sure-enough rain before I was long on the road. Good for crops—a dry June meant scanty harvests or no harvests at all—but not so good for deputy sheriffs. Yet I was pleased with it. A predictable climate was no climate for me. What if we were having a late spring or, rather, a late early summer? What if the pasque-flowers had come and gone? The gold of balsamroot was showing and the purple-blue of lupine, and other blooms would follow. The rain ensured that prediction.

I drove up along the Rose and visited the cabin, the slicker draining off some of the rain. A side window had been broken and the sash lifted. I entered that way. Inside was, if not a shambles, then a mess, in the kitchen particularly. Boxes and cans, pots and pans had been taken from cabinets and shelves and thrown on the floor. But things of ready value, like binoculars and rifles, had been left hanging. Kids' work, all right, and the kids were probably hunting for booze. Not knowing the inventory, I couldn't tell whether any had been stolen. Fingerprints wouldn't help me, or footprints, either. How check out every youngster in town or be sure local kids were involved?

On a bench were a hammer, nails and a saw and, outside, some discarded planks. It might not have been in the line of duty, but I boarded up the broken window, through which the rain had started to blow. Maybe the owner would thank the office for keeping out pack rats, water and dust.

My work surely justified lunch on the house. I found crackers and a can of sardines.

Not until early afternoon did I get to the Bar Star. It was a dull hour, and Tad Frazier had nothing to do except polish glasses he'd already polished. I told him there might be a job for him in the sheriff's office.

"How much?" he asked, looking interested.

"You'll have to talk to Sheriff Charleston about that. I'm not making an offer. It's just a possibility."

"I'll see him," he said. "You know I couldn't go to work right away. I'd want to give proper notice. I hope the sheriff will understand?"

"He will. He'll take due notice as a recommendation."

We had got that far, which was far enough, when Halvor Amussen came in. I asked him if he wanted relief.

"That's nice, Hawkshaw," he said. "Maybe tonight. No, tomorrow night. This job gets in the way of my private business."

I knew he meant he had little time to court his true love.

I drove to the office to relieve Jimmy. "Got his nose in a book," Jimmy said with a glance toward the inner office. "Good thing the taxpayers don't know how busy we are."

There were only three or four calls, none important. One was from the old lady who was always hearing hounds howl. Not so this time. A couple of them had got stuck in her front yard. She didn't use those words, but that's what she meant. I told her someone would be along within half an hour. I didn't tell her that nature would remove the disgrace in the meantime.

At five o'clock Jimmy and Inspector Gewald came in together. Gewald marched to the inner door and opened it without knocking. I followed him, hoping Charleston had put his book away. He had.

"Well, Mr. Gewald," Charleston said as Gewald took a chair, "I hope you found something to help us."

"Very little," Gewald answered, holding his hat tight in his lap. "Nothing to do with the present case or, rather, cases."

"But?"

"You are allowing a house of prostitution to operate." The words came out as an indictment. He could be talking only about Jessie Lou.

"Is that so? You have the evidence? Witnesses, including yourself? A base for a charge?"

"Naturally not. A little vigilance would establish the fact. I said *fact.*" The fact revolted him. It made his mouth small.

"We are involved in murders, Mr. Gewald."

"All crime is important."

Charleston bent forward over his desk, his expression humorless. "You are a member of the attorney general's department. The house, if there is one, is the proper concern of the county attorney, you must know that much. See him."

"I'll do just that, and tomorrow I'm going out to interview those two squaws."

"You might. I won't," I said. "Tomorrow's the day of the funeral."

Charleston told him, "You'll be on your own."

Gewald clamped on his hat, rose and marched out.

I knew what Charleston was going to say before he said it. The word was "pisswillie."

Mother had fixed fried chicken, mashed potatoes, gravy, biscuits and a salad that night. Her fried chicken was better than any other, home-done or commercial, and she considered it a disgrace if even one lump were found in her mashed potatoes.

My father was in a good mood, partly from the food and partly, I imagined, because Brother Sam had folded his tent the week before. After eating, the three of us stayed in the kitchen and talked about this and that, including the fact that, from appearances, I might never have been clobbered by Luke McGluke.

"You know," I said during a pause, "I think I'd like to take some courses in criminology, if I can find any."

"And become a policeman?" Father asked.

"A detective, maybe."

"Or a small-town sheriff?"

"Not so much, but I wouldn't mind being like Mr. Charleston. He's more than a sheriff."

Father smiled his little, twisted smile of agreement. "He certainly is."

Mother said, "Whatever you do, you'll be a good man, Jase. Mr. Charleston certainly is no bad example."

We left my suggestion there.

Father went into the living room and found the book he had started. I helped Mother with the dishes and thought about refreshing my neglected knowledge of fingerprinting, but decided not to. We had no case that seemed to call for that skill. So I took a bath and changed clothes.

At ten-thirty I was lounging in the neighborhood of the Commercial Cafe, trying not to be conspicuous while I waited for Jessie Lou to finish her shift. It had quit raining, and the air smelled of summer hope. I had to linger for half an hour.

She didn't see me at first or anything else but her shoes and the sidewalk. One step and another, leading to nowhere. She seemed startled when I said, "Jessie Lou."

She lifted a tired face. "Oh, hello, Jase."

"Do you mind if I walk you home?"

"For what?"

"I have to talk to you."

She turned. "We'll walk the other way, then."

Except for some voices sounding from the Bar Star, the street was silent. No one but us walked along it.

After a while she said, "When you and the others were at lunch, I gave you a look. Did you know I wanted to see you?"

"I guess maybe so, but the shoe's on the other foot now."

"Meaning?"

I plunged right in. "There's a state snoop in town. He knows about you and your house. It's none of his business, the damn buttinsky, but he's out to get you."

"He's been listening to ancient history."

It was my turn to ask what was meant.

"I gave it up, Jase. I'll keep slinging hash. I'll sling hash
the rest of my life." There was such despair in her voice
as to wring any man's heart.

So I was gruff. "Gave it up? Gave it up when?"

"If you have to know, it was right after our date, if you
want to call it that. No more, I said to myself." Her words
came slow, forlorn but somehow firm, as if she had had to
pick one of two bad choices and had done so, knowing the
cost. "No more it has been, and no more it will be. Not for
money. Never again." She looked up, and in the darkness
I could see she was trying to smile. "That's that."

"So you didn't and don't need my warning?"

She didn't answer, and we walked on, stepping slow. I
heard her take a breath. She said, "But there's still what
I wanted to tell you about."

"Please do. What is it?"

"Dave Becker."

"Becker? He's out of town."

"He wasn't. He followed me home last night and tried
to force himself on me. I wouldn't do it, Jase. Whatever
I've been, I couldn't bring myself to. That man! To go to
bed with him? It would have been—well, I thought it
would be like the touch of oysters on the skin." She
paused. "He roughed me up some, but he didn't get what
he wanted. I'm proud of that."

I said, "I'm proud of you, but I don't see what I can do.
I don't see that it gets us anywhere much."

She went on in that small, sad voice. "But that's not all.
I'm not quite sure of what I'm going to say. I couldn't
really swear to it. But while he was arguing with me and

mauling me, I got an idea. He didn't say it in so many words, not out and out, but my idea was that he was trying to deal with Eagle Charlie so as to sleep with Rosa once in a while."

"All the same Grimsley?" I said. "Just what did he say?"

"Jase, I was being shouted at and knocked around, and how can I remember exactly? I know he mentioned Eagle Charlie, and I know he mentioned Rosa, pitting her against me, I guess you could say. He was mad, and he didn't talk too much sense."

"If he did make a deal—"

"But he didn't. That's the important thing. That's what I gathered. That's what made him sore, one of the things. Maybe Rosa objected. Maybe they couldn't agree on a price. I think it was price. I know that Becker was damning Eagle Charlie to hell."

I said, "Oh, boy!"

"Does it help? Tell me."

"Maybe more than you can imagine. Thanks isn't a good-enough word."

"Then I'm glad."

"Now can I take you home?"

"Just down to the crossing, Jase. No farther, please."

At the intersection I gave her a quick kiss and said, "Thanks, and be proud, Jessie Lou."

I watched the small figure retreat down the street. It looked lonely and friendless and without hope. A hasher, forever?

What I had learned was too good to keep, I thought. The time was midnight, but still I called Charleston from our street telephone booth. He answered at once. The man might seem relaxed, but he never seemed sleepy.

I told him what I had learned, not mentioning Jessie Lou by name. I heard the intake of his breath.

He said, "Things move along, Jase, thanks to you and your secret operative. See you in the morning. It was your operative, wasn't it?"

"Yes, sir."

"Jase, you didn't—?"

"I did not." I spoke with force, but ended on a fool note. "Besides, she's not doing it anymore."

"Good boy," Charleston said, "and good night."

Chapter
Fourteen

CHARLESTON was on the phone when I pushed into the inner office the next morning. "Yes, Mrs. Lindstrom," he was saying, "we'll certainly try to find her. I'll notify surrounding authorities and the newspaper. Two or three days, you say? If you could bring in a picture of your daughter, it would help. Her age? Yes, I have it. Sixteen."

He said to me as he put the phone back. "Missing girl, name of Linda Lindstrom, juvenile. Parents! They're not even sure how long she's been gone. How she was dressed."

He had hardly hung up when another call came, relayed through Jimmy. He listened, got up abruptly and said, "Come on. A bad wreck on the Titus road."

On the way out he told Jimmy, "You heard? Notify the highway patrol, Doc Yak and Felix."

"Soon as you quit talkin'," Jimmy said. His hand was already on the dial.

We climbed in the Special and drove away, the tires screeching at turns. "Two kids, both hurt," he said. "Maybe dead. One-car accident. It happened near Fred Harris's place. He made the call."

"No identification?"

"He couldn't say. Said they missed a curve, hit a telephone pole, turned over and landed right side up, maybe not in that order."

He sounded the siren and shot past a car. In the siren's dying wail he said, "Mix kids, alcohol and wheels, cook on an open road, and take out the cake."

The tires squealed as we braked at the scene. A car, its front end and top mashed in, stood in an unfenced field off the road. Farther on, a shattered telephone pole hung by its wires. A highway patrol cruiser was already on hand. A girl hunched near, screaming.

The patrolman was Sven Svenson, whom we knew. He was a good officer. He was peering inside the door of the wreck. When he saw us, he turned and approached.

"Howdy. Just happened by," he informed us. "The boy at the wheel looks hurt bad."

"Doctor's on the way," Charleston said.

The girl was pacing back and forth, crying out, "Oh, God, I'm going to die. I hurt. Help me, Jesus! Help, someone!"

"Thrown clear, I would say," Svenson said with distaste.

Charleston went to her. "Be quiet! Hush up! What's your name?"

"I'm dying."

"You're not. Name, please?"

"God save me! God save poor Linda!"

"Linda Lindstrom?"

"It was. It was. It was." She collapsed by the roadside and moaned. She could have been pretty, I thought, grade-school pretty, but now her clothes were dirty and torn, and her face swollen and red, like a man's marked by booze.

A man I had hardly noticed stood at the other side of the road. He came closer and said his name was Fred Harris. Damn shame, young people and cars.

The long cry of the ambulance sounded and died hard. The ambulance braked to a stop. Doc Yak, following close, bumped it and scrambled out.

Some traffic was beginning to build up, both ways. Drivers and passengers peered through the opened windows. Some of them got out but stayed at a distance. Blood attracted people but still held them back. Another patrolman, probably the one Jimmy called, was trying to steer the traffic on by. It didn't like to move.

I walked with Doc and Felix to the wreck. So did Charleston and Svenson. From the first look I had, I thought the boy driver might already be dead. He drooped against the wheel, his face bloody, his head bashed. Felix unfolded his stretcher.

Doc made a quick examination, mostly just a feeling for pulse. "Might live," he said.

The girl had got to her feet and come close. Her screams hurt my ears. "I'm dying. I'm going to die. Tell me the truth, Doctor, I'm about dead."

Doc Yak turned on her, his expression wicked. "Shut up! You won't die unless somebody kills you." He flourished his stethoscope. "It might be me."

We had to yank at the car door. It came open with a screech of tortured metal.

Doc Yak had said, "He won't get well in there." Now he told us, "Ease him out. Easy. Careful, now."

It was Charleston, Svenson and I who gentled the body out and laid it on the stretcher. I saw one leg was angled as no well leg could be.

Doc Yak made a second examination, more thorough but hasty. "Put him in the ambulance."

"Just a minute, Doc," Svenson said. "Identification. Can you manage to get his wallet, any papers?"

Doc looked displeased but came up with the wallet.

Charleston, Felix and I carried the stretcher to the ambulance and slid it inside. Carrying it, I noticed what I must have noticed before. The boy smelled rank, as if he had been dipped in a vat.

As a sort of parting shot to the world, Doc Yak said, "Damn fool kids! Nothing but appetites. Nothing but goddamn glands." Then, to the waiting girl, who was only crying now, "Get in! Get in with your heart's desire. I'll examine you at the office."

Not for the first time, then, I saw the other side of Doc Yak. He climbed into the ambulance himself, the better to stave off death. His car stood abandoned. Felix managed to turn the ambulance around and, with the patrolman's help, roll by the traffic. I went to Doc's car, found the key in it and drove it off the road.

Charleston and Svenson had gone to inspect the wreck. From it Charleston removed four bottles, one half full. Three, including the half-full one, were fifths of whiskey. They bore the label, OLD ROSCOE CROMWELL. The one that had held wine said, "Bottled Especially for Roscoe Cromwell."

Looking at them, Charleston said, "No telling how many they ditched." An expression of vague dislike came to his face. "A real card, that Roscoe Cromwell. A really funny man."

Svenson was examining the wallet. "The kid had a driver's license, if it's his. Name of Joseph J. Hanks, age nineteen. He lives in Titus, and the car's registered in that county, so it's maybe not hot. I'll get hold of his parents, or try to." He looked over the scene and the car and made some notes.

He managed to open the back door opposite that through which Charleston had taken the bottles. "Look at this mess," he said while Charleston nodded. "Tissue wipers, soiled. Half-eaten sandwiches. Spills of booze." He pulled out a rumpled blanket. With a good officer's distaste for untidiness he went on, "Christ, not even sanitary. See? They've been high-balling around, drinking and diddling, enjoying the best things in life, and to hell with cleaning up."

Charleston said, "The girl's under age, reported missing just this morning. The bottles were stolen from a summer cabin. We know that much. So it's breaking and entering, contributing to delinquency, larceny."

Svenson put his notebook in his pocket. "Besides driving while drunk."

The other patrolman, having straightened out the traffic, had come up. He stood listening.

Svenson half-smiled. "You won't have to worry that Hanks might skip. He'll be around for a while. Here, you want this?"

He offered the blanket to Charleston, who took it between his thumb and one finger. I did the same when he handed it to me. "Put it in the car, will you, Jase? The bottles, too."

After I'd done so, we said good-bye to the patrolmen and made for the Special. A car had been pulled off the road behind it. A couple of men moved closer to us, and one of them asked, "How bad, Sheriff?"

"Bad enough. Ask Doc Yak, George."

Once we were under way, I said, "Two cases solved, anyhow. Missing girl. Break-in. Quick, too."

"One thing and another. One interruption after another. The life of the law. Start after a wolf and find yourself chasing a rabbit. And just as I get an idea about our two murders, here, on top of other bothers, here comes Mr. Upright and louses things up."

"You can't just ignore Mr. Gewald?"

"Not very well, Jase. I can't say scat to a state inspector." He sighed. "Well, I'll let him play out his string."

"You've almost talked me out of it," I said. "I was thinking about taking some courses in criminology. What about that?"

"If you want to, why not? That's the only advice I can give you. Not that advice would do you any good. In the end all decisions come from inside." He took his eyes off the road and gave me a smile.

He pulled the car in at the front of Doc Yak's office. Only Doc's office girl was inside, and she wasn't a girl but a woman of spreading middle age. Charleston asked her, "No Doc?"

"No Doc, Chick. He and Felix took off with that hurt boy, bound for the city and the hospital."

"What about the girl, Dotty?"

"Linda Lindstrom. Just shaken up. Halvor Amussen took her in charge." Her head moved in sympathy. "He's got his hands full."

Charleston said thanks, and we drove to the office. It might have been the arrival room at an insane asylum. Linda had the shrieks again, and Halvor was trying to soothe her. I figured she wasn't finding much comfort there, not in an ox however well-meaning.

We took them in as we stood at the opened door. Jimmy was saying, while the girl squawked, "Amussen, for God's sake make her shut up! Slap her down! Throw her into a cell! Do something!"

Linda threw herself on a chair and put her hands to her face. "Slap me, then. Kill me. What do I care? I'm bad hurt, and you just stand there. You want me to die."

Jimmy said, "That's a pretty fair guess."

Halvor made a cooing sound and tried a pat on her shoulder. She didn't buy either.

Charleston strode forward, took one hand from her face and slapped her. Then he slapped her on the other side. "Come out of it! Come out of it this minute!"

She looked at him unbelieving, her mouth open. "You hit me!"

"Medicine," he said. "Cure for hysteria."

Halvor asked, "No charge?"

"It's a juvenile case. Judge Todd's baby."

"I already called him," Halvor said.

"What about her parents? Did you phone them?"

"No. I wasn't sure."

Charleston said, "Good. The office is madhouse enough as it is. Drive her home, Jase."

The girl was only whimpering now. She let me lead her to the county car and got in without fuss. She even told me how to get to her home, which was fifteen miles out. The whimpers died. Her eyes stared ahead, out of a sullen face, a hung-over face. She stank with stale drink.

By and by she moved closer to me. "I don't want to go home. Please don't take me there."

"That's where you belong. I'm under orders."

A hand touched my shoulder. "I'll give you anything if you don't, anything I have."

"No deal, Linda. And you better guide me there right. Hear?"

"My old man will probably be drunk," she said in a little girl's voice. "He's mean when he's drunk."

"What about your mother?"

"She doesn't need to be drunk, not to be mean. Whatever I tell them, they'll give me hell."

I supposed she was right. They'd give her hell. What she might not have realized was that she was giving them hell in her turn. I said, "Tit for tat," and let the subject rest there.

I helped her out of the car and took her arm as she dragged to the door of home. A stout woman appeared in the entrance, her hands on her hips.

I told her, "We found your girl for you."

I might not have been there. She said, "You come in, young lady! You come right in." Her voice sounded like metal being sawed.

I didn't want to hear any more. I climbed in the car and drove back.

One thing and another, Charleston had said. Today was the day for it.

Entering the office as I walked toward it were Inspector Gewald, Pambrun and Framboise. He was herding them ahead of him.

The door was still open when I reached it, and Jimmy's voice was saying, "I don't care who in hell you are. No more charging into the sheriff's office. What you do is ask me will he see you, and I call and find out. Learn some manners."

Gewald said, "Call him then."

Jimmy didn't have to. Charleston came out.

"I rounded up these two after the funeral," Gewald

informed him. "Tomorrow I'll get the squaws. I want some questions answered."

"We'll go into the spare room," Charleston said, and I knew he was giving Gewald, if not short shrift, something close to it. The spare room was seldom used except for reference. It had files in it mostly, but a desk and chairs, too. "Come on. You, too, Jase."

There were just chairs enough.

Gewald addressed Charleston. "You told me these two men found the body?"

"That's right."

"So we ask some more questions."

Neither Pambrun nor Framboise had said a word. They perched on their seats, glancing quick at each other.

"They're clean," Charleston said. "We questioned them. It's in our reports."

"I'll do my own investigating, if you don't mind. Yours seems not to have led anywhere."

Charleston only sighed. I smiled at the two men, hoping to cheer them.

Gewald switched around to face them. "So you found the body of Eagle Charlie, huh? How come? What were you doing?"

"Just walking outside," Pambrun answered. "It was morning. We were first to get up. We always are. So there was Eagle Charlie, dead. So tell the sheriff. That's what we did."

"You might have thought that was pretty cute—to kill the man and then report to the sheriff. Who would suspect you?"

"It was the right thing," Framboise said. "You find a dead man, you tell the law."

"After making sure he was dead?"

The point was lost on Pambrun. "He was dead, all right. We found that out."

"You ever been in trouble with the law?"

They both shook their heads.

I had to break in then. "Look, Mr. Gewald. I know these men. They are my friends. They are my father's friends. They're all right."

"I find your character references less than convincing," Gewald said. If he could have snorted with that thin nose and tight mouth, he would have.

He addressed the two men again. "How do you know you were first up?"

"No one around," Pambrun said. "No one else."

"But if it wasn't you, it must have been somebody else, somebody there before you. What do you say to that?"

Framboise replied, "Maybe so. We see no one."

"More questions, Mr. Gewald?" Charleston inquired.

"Sure. I want to know about relationships." He spoke now to the breeds. "What did you have against Eagle Charlie?"

With their eyes the two consulted before Pambrun answered. "Nothing. What for we have anything against him?"

Framboise added, "Not against him. For him. Thanks. He let us stay there. We use his water, free. When he had plenty meat, he gave us some. Why kill him?"

"That's what I'm trying to find out."

"Not from us," Pambrun told him. "Nothing."

"Not a little bit something," Framboise said.

"What about the old squaw? What's her name? Old Woman Gray Wolf. She quarreled with Eagle Charlie."

"She fussed. Him and her fussed. That's all," Framboise answered.

"You tell me she wouldn't kill him?"

Pambrun shrugged. "What for? So she could starve. Herself, nothing, that's all she had."

"Maybe. We'll see what she says."

Framboise might have smiled. "Sure. Ask her. Spend plenty time asking her."

Gewald threw an inquiring glance at Charleston. It wasn't answered. Now Gewald took another tack. "Let's say you're innocent. Let's say she is. Then who wanted to kill Eagle Charlie? Who in fact did?"

Pambrun answered this time. "Who knows? Not us. Sure thing not us."

"Anything more, Mr. Gewald?" Charleston asked.

"Not for now," Gewald said through his close lips. "I may want to question them again later."

I accompanied the two men to their old car. "I hope you don't blame us," I told them on the way. "That Gewald is a load. We have to carry it for a while."

They let themselves smile, and Pambrun said, "Buck him off."

At nine o'clock that night I relieved Amussen and cruised around town until the bars closed. It had been a long day.

Chapter
Fifteen

"HE'S THE STONE we've left unturned," Charleston said
to me. He was talking about Red Fall.

We were driving west, to Guy Jamison's dude ranch.
The morning was clear and soft, kind as a caress too long
forgotten. Before us the mountains lifted, sharp as knife
cuts. Through the rear window the sun was telling us that
all was all right. It might be, if only long enough to make
a man forgive our climate.

"Even if there's nothing under the stone," I said, "at
least we're away from Inspector Gewald."

"That was part of my idea," Charleston said, smiling.
"We'll let him investigate all he wants to. He has the
Indian women to question. Maybe Luke McGluke, too.
God knows who else. He hasn't even looked at our re-
ports, which may be just as well. So we stand by. We give
him free rein. He just might come up with something.
Who knows? Remember, he's a determined man."

"Rigid."

"That and ambitious."

I said, "Righteous, too. From what I know, he ought to
team up with Red Fall."

We drove along, content with an easy speed. On the
rocky slopes to either side the carpet flowers welcomed

our coming. I thought they might not like to blush unseen.

"One dividend," Charleston said presently. "We'll have a good lunch. Guy insisted we stay for it."

"I can eat it. Fall in on the party?"

"He'll show up later."

The road rose to the foothills. As it climbed, we entered a land of rock, patches of creeping juniper and jack pines. The pines grew tortured, deformed but defiant of the wild winds from the west. Endurance, I thought, hardihood. Against all the odds they survived. They hung tight to home.

We entered the Rose River canyon. Here the cliffs, rising sheer, closed in on us. They were craggy-faced, ominous in the eyes of those who knew only flatlands. Even so, here and there in crevice and cranny jack pines found foothold.

The cliffs opened into a park, and there was the dude ranch with smoke rising from a chimney. I could smell the good smell of woodsmoke. Wild clover grew on this little flat, and native grasses. A milk cow grazed there. The buildings stood tidy and solid, old ones and new included. Two horses looked at us from a corral.

Guy Jamison, usually busy in workshop, cabins or corral, was waiting for us at the door of the lodge. He came out toward the car and said welcome. We shook his hand. "Come in," he said. "Happy to see you."

The lodge room always filled me with admiration. The walls were of logs, close-fitted, barked, maybe stained a little and sealed. The furniture—chairs, sofas and tables— were all handmade, of a design and quality never available in any store. The hardware was a home product, too. Its black contrasted with the native tones of the wood.

Guy Jamison was more than a dude rancher: he was an artist.

Almost as soon as we sat down, Mrs. Jamison came in with a coffee tray. She was a small woman, close on middle age, whose energy, I knew, exceeded her size by about ten to one. Noticing that I had looked around, Jamison said, "Grandpa sleeps a lot."

Over coffee we talked of the dude season, of cows and grass and markets and the prospect for crops. Charleston seemed content to ignore the subject of first interest. Before lunch Jamison mixed drinks for us. It was then that he said, "Fall's fixing fence on the south field. He took his lunch with him. He'll be through by three o'clock or thereabouts."

"No great hurry," Charleston answered.

"It's none of my business, but I don't know why you want to see him?"

"To find if he can help us in naming a murderer. We've questioned everyone else, everyone we could think of."

"I understand, but I would bet you don't turn up anything. He's a good man. Hard worker. Tidy, too. He has quarters here, you know, and even my wife can't find fault with the way he keeps house."

"Has he spent much time here?"

"He's here when I want him. Of course I haven't had much work for him. Too early. Be a week or so before the first dudes arrive."

"It's the Breedtown angle," Charleston said. "On his visits there he might have learned something, something he doesn't know is significant."

"Maybe. I doubt it. His interest is in that old squaw and what she can tell him. You ought to see the notes he's

taken about Indian ways and beliefs. Piled up, they're
knee-high. If you get him started, he'll chew your ears off.
He's a religious boy, you know. Educated, to boot."

Mrs. Jamison came from the kitchen to say lunch was
ready. The dining area was just off the lodge room. It had
a fireplace in it, chairs and a sideboard. The table was long
enough to seat twenty or thirty guests. We ate at one end
of it.

You can figure on good meals at dude ranches. The
guests would quit coming otherwise. I knew that, season
after season, the Jamisons had repeaters. This day we ate
tenderloin steaks, homemade rolls, plain boiled cabbage
boiled just enough and a fruit salad. Dessert? Why, sure
thing. It was nutcake with whipped cream.

After coffee Charleston lit a cigar and Jamison fash-
ioned a cigarette, using Bull Durham. The talk was
relaxed, easy, not to any point much. Each of us carried
his plate to the kitchen, Mrs. Jamison protesting.

"Maybe you'd like to walk around for a while," Jamison
suggested. "Waiting gets tiresome. But, if you want to, I'll
ride over and get Fall now."

"Don't do that," Charleston said.

So we took a tour, looking into cabins, at each item of
improvement. We strolled to the corral and took note of
the horses.

"Mixed breed," Jamison said. "Mostly quarter horses
crossed with Tennessee Walker. They're best for the
mountains, I've found. They step right out and don't tire
like some. Fall or I will bring in the whole bunch before
long."

Just to show interest, I asked, "How many do you
have?"

"About sixty, counting some pack mules. Fall knows how to handle mules. He used to work with burros, you know. Claims they can outpack and outwear horses or mules, either one. He thinks I ought to buy some."

"They're mighty small," Charleston said.

"That's what I tell him. He may be right about strength and all, but he's not used to packing on trails like ours. Hell, they'd high-center on deadfall."

We walked back to the house and had a beer, and before long Fall showed up. Obviously he had taken time to freshen up. His shoulder-length hair was combed, and his shirt and pants just back from the washer. He shook hands and said it was a pleasure to see us.

After a few bits of conversation Jamison excused himself, saying, "I'll leave you to talk while I tend to some things." What he was tending to was good manners.

Fall said, "I'll help you later."

"No need today. Tomorrow maybe you can finish the fencing?"

"I'll do that."

With Jamison gone, I butted my chair back a little way from Charleston and Fall and tried not to make a show of my notebook.

Charleston began formally. "Mr. Fall, you may be able to help us. We hope so."

"Certainly. In any manner I can."

"It's about the two murders, of course. First, F. Y. Grimsley and then Eagle Charlie. By the way, did you know Grimsley?"

"Only to see him. We never met. We never talked to each other."

"I was pretty sure of that. It's about Eagle Charlie that we think you might help us. You did know him?"

"I talked to him a time or two and saw him off and on. We weren't close, ever."

"You visited Breedtown pretty often. Right?"

The sun, sinking toward the mountains, got returning flashes from Fall's red hair. "I suppose you could call it often. I've been there several times. Mrs. Gray Wolf interests me."

"In what way?"

"She's a repository of her tribe's almost-lost beliefs, one of the last ones. You may know I'm doing research?"

"So I've heard."

"I've interviewed the oldest members of other tribes, both men and women, here and south of here. I may have enough material for a book." Eagerness came into his voice. "Would you like to see some of my notes?"

"I would, but I'm afraid we haven't time for that now." Charleston took a couple of cigars from his pocket and offered Fall one. It was declined. "Did Mrs. Gray Wolf talk directly to you?"

"Never in our interviews. She could do it, I think, but she wouldn't. She's returned to her past, rejecting assimilation and any degree of it. I rather admire her."

I rather admired Fall's language. He never learned it wrangling dudes.

"You talked through an interpreter, then?" Charleston said.

"Yes, of course. Through Mrs. Charlie, who is versed in both tongues."

Some ornery impulse prompted me to say "She's quite a dish."

Fall gave me a look. "If that's what you call human beings of the opposite sex."

I was squelched into silence.

Charleston came in with "Let's digress a minute. I'm interested in your research, the purposes of it. I don't mean to diminish your studies. I just want to know more about them."

He had opened the gate. Fall surged through it. "I'd like to tell you, Mr. Charleston, all that I can in the time we have. So. It is both astonishing and heartening that the sense of God abides, it seems, in all men, red, white and other colors, though of the latter I can't speak with certain knowledge. Certainly it's true of the tribes I know. There are differences from Christian doctrine, of course, but the mystery of God, the divine mystery, is everywhere, not only in the universe but in the minds of men. There is no disputing it. That will be my theme."

"An overall sense of divinity, even among those we call savages or pagans? I wouldn't argue the point. But what about superstitions foreign to our thinking?"

"You find them, I grant. Childish things, though, not so deeply felt, not so embracing, as the sense we are speaking of. It took Jesus Christ to awaken and activate our brooding knowledge. It is for us, those so blessed as to know Him, to teach what He taught us."

Fall took a breath and proceeded, if anything more earnest and intent than before. Despite myself, I was impressed by his convictions and his ability to state them. "There, I am sure, the missionaries have failed or at most only partly succeeded. They should have known and acknowledged the universal and fundamental belief in God. Instead, they introduced God as a foreign deity, a presence and power imposed from outside by outsiders. Yet He was there, the recognition of Him was there all the time. He was their own."

Charleston studied the words and studied the speaker. Rather abruptly, I thought, he asked, "Why do you wrangle dudes?"

Fall let himself smile, now that he was diverted. He made a little wave with an open hand. "What better way to keep close to your subject and still make money to live on? I'm not making a career of it."

Charleston said, "That's answer enough. Now, Mr. Fall, to get to our problem. Does your experience at Breedtown bring you to suspect anybody? Was anything said, anything done to your knowledge, anything that might give us a clue?"

Fall shook his head. His tone was regretful. "I'm afraid not."

I broke in with "Old Woman Gray Wolf hated Eagle Charlie, didn't she?"

"I guess she didn't like him, but she wouldn't have murdered him. Of that I'm sure. She is a Christian lady, Indian but Christian and a lady. I promise you that."

"Was she acquainted with Grimsley?"

"You'll have to ask her. I don't know."

"Have you any reason to suspect Luke McGluke?"

"Heavens, no. That poor man." Fall turned to me. "His fight with you, his use of a rock, that was all a mistake. He was frightened out of what wits he has."

"So we discovered," Charleston said. "So you know nothing that might help us?"

"I told you before, I don't have a hint. I'm suspicious of no one. You must consider, though, that my interest hasn't been in crime. It is in the beliefs, the aspirations of man. In that single purpose I may have failed to note what you might think important."

Charleston smiled and said, "A sheriff's work hardly permits that single line. We'll go now, but thank you."

We rose and went to the door. Neither of our hosts was in sight, outside or in, so we had to postpone our thanks to them.

While we had been talking, the weather had turned. A cold wind shrilled down the canyon, as if to remind us not to take the climate for granted. Going to the car, we had to hang on to our hats.

On the way home I asked Charleston, "Nothing there I could see. You?"

"I forgot to ask where he was educated."

"Is that important?"

"Not a damn bit," Charleston answered and fell silent.

Chapter
Sixteen

THAT NIGHT the wind died and rain came.

Rain? We called it a cloudburst. The annual precipitation in our country averages out under fourteen inches. A three-day rain may measure no more than an inch and a fraction, and here, in five hours, four inches pelted down before nature decided to slack off and merely soak roots, not wash gullies.

The pounding on the roof woke me up. I couldn't tell what time it was, looking through the window. What I saw through the blurred pane was an obscuring sheet like a waterfall.

I shaved and put on my clothes and went to the kitchen. My father and mother were already up. The room smelled of fresh coffee and frying bacon.

"You're surely not working today, Jase," my father said.

"I'm afraid so. Anyhow, who can sleep when a rain like this beats the roof?"

"We couldn't," Mother put in, while she broke an egg in the pan.

Father, seated at the table, tried to see out the window. He said, "All aboard for Mount Ararat." He turned to me. "I'll drive you to work when you're ready, Jase. But Mr. Charleston ought to provide you a car."

"No, Dad. He's scrupulous about charging mileage, about private use."

"Good thing on the whole."

We had plenty of time over breakfast. The morning had lightened a little, as if the sun was up there somewhere. I was putting on a yellow slicker, complete with hood, when a horn sounded outside. Charleston was there, waiting for me. I opened the car door and said, "Good taxicab service."

"Almost missed my fare," Charleston told me with a smile. "Two bridges about to wash out. I brought Geet in and dropped her off at the apartment. Didn't want her marooned." He sobered. "With all that snow in the mountains, it could be a sure-enough flood."

Gewald was already in the office when we entered, dripping. He was polite enough to say "Good morning."

As we took off our slickers and hung them up, Charleston answered, "Good and wet."

"I don't let the weather deter me. Can't. It's a full-time business, enforcement is."

Charleston eased himself into a chair, and I took mine. "Never cry uncle, that's our motto," Charleston said. His eyes, not his mouth, smiled at me.

"I'm going to Breedtown for those two women." Gewald's gaze was inquiring, as if he hoped for an offer of help. Charleston didn't volunteer. Neither did I.

"Go ahead and try, if you're bound to," Charleston informed him, "but you'll never make it."

Gewald found it hard to believe. "How can you be sure about that?"

"Part of the road is gravel and dirt, or it was. Now it's hub-deep mud. There's a stream to cross, too, a dinky stream in dry weather. By this time it's likely a torrent."

Gewald seemed convinced if still doubtful. "There's other fish still to fry." He rose, took his slicker and rain hat off a hook and put them on. They were black. He went out.

Charleston took a deep breath and let it out slowly. "Dedication, Jase. That's his name. That's where we fall down. Not enough purpose."

"Mine's kind of drowned out today. From the look of things it won't make shore very soon."

Charleston nodded agreeably, lifted the phone and spoke to Jimmy. "Still out of commission, huh?"

After he put the phone back, he said, "Jimmy's been trying to ring the Chuck Cleaver ranch, last night and this morning, as I asked him to. No luck. All the country phones are out of order, mine included. What I want to know is, is Dave Becker back." He looked with distaste on a clutter of papers on his desk. "I have to get this stuff out of the way. No dedication on account of paper work. Piss-willie. But, Jase, you might take the county car and see if you can get to Chuck Cleaver's. Just find out if Becker is there. Nothing else."

I was willing if not eager.

Jimmy looked at me as I paused at the door. "Even a goddamn duck takes shelter in weather like this."

"I want to know where they find it."

"I'll crank up by and by and meet you in my new launch."

The rain was still pouring down. The gutters were full, some overflowing. No life showed in the streets, and no lights. I caught a glimpse of Felix Underwood's face at a window. He might have been thinking it was good

weather for drownings but poor for graveside services.
The Bar Star sat like a relic of a ghost town.

The road to the north narrowed once it entered the
country. The borrow pits swam. I came to the Excelsior
Ditch, the biggest irrigation ditch out of the Rose River,
and to the bridge that formerly spanned it. The ditch was
a river and had carried the bridge out to sea or wherever.
A big truck loaded with lumber stood at the side of the
road. Near it was a pickup. A man left the pickup, scurried
to my car and got in without invitation. His name was Joe
Talbey. He was a solid-built man with a nose flattened in
his days as a brawler. His slicker dripped on cushion and
floor. He said, "Holy Jesus and then some."

"Hi, Joe. Double or triple whatever it is."

One hand burrowed inside his clothes and came out
with a cigarette and matches. After lighting up and taking
a drag, he said, "Thanks for a roof over my head. That old
pickup leaks like a sieve."

"Who's with you?"

"Two of 'em, snug over in the big truck. There's just
three of us altogether and not near enough. Not enough
equipment, either. But the boss tells us to haul ass. He was
afraid the bridge might go out like it has once before.
Smart man that way, but Christ. Half the river's comin'
down that goddamn ditch and more to come, and he
wants us to repair it, and today is Sunday to boot."

I hadn't thought about the day of the week. The office
didn't keep careful track because crime didn't, either.

Joe said, "How you goin' to do it, Jase? How you goin'
to bridge that crazy water?"

"Pontoons. They're the ticket."

A puff of smoke came out as he smiled. "Sure, and I

never took thought. The shop's crowded with the damn things. War surplus, you know."

"No way around?" I asked, knowing there wasn't any quick way and perhaps no way at all.

"If you want to drive a hundred miles from up on the bench, then maybe so. Me, I'm going home." He left me, the cigarette in his mouth. The rain would snuff it soon enough.

I managed to turn the county car around. The rain, though slackened, kept me company back to the office, where I arrived wet and dirty from the pleasant business of changing a tire.

Jimmy was busy on the telephone. "Just a minute," he said, turning to me. "How about the road north?"

"No go. The Excelsior bridge is out and maybe others farther on."

"Don't try it," Jimmy said into the telephone. "Bridges washed out. You're welcome."

Jimmy hung up the phone and told me, "We're shut off to the south, too. I got that from the highway patrol. The only route out of this swamp is the Titus road." The telephone rang. "Christ, all these calls!"

Charleston was making headway on his paper work. It appeared he might be half finished. He raised his head as I entered. "I couldn't make it," I informed him. "The Excelsior bridge is washed out, and the ditch a long way out of its banks. There's no possible ford."

"I was afraid so." His gaze went over me. "You had some trouble?"

"A flat."

He seemed disgusted, with himself or circumstance. "Remind me, Jase, we need new tires on that car. Why don't you go home and clean up? Use the car. You look as if you'd just crawled out of a beaver house."

I said, "Thanks, Mr. Charleston. What about later?"

"It's Sunday. If you feel like it, see if you can pick up something in town, anything at all. You don't have to, though. It's just a suggestion. Got that?"

"I'll feel like it," I answered. "Could I ask what goes with Mr. Gewald?"

"You can ask, but I can't answer. He left. He's still gone." He smiled a tired smile. Paper work always made him fretful. "No doubt he's collared the guilty man."

I drove home through the diminishing rain.

"You go right in and take a hot bath," Mother said after one look at me. "You ought not to go out in weather like this. You shouldn't have to. Doesn't Mr. Charleston know that? Go on. I'll get a quick snack ready for you."

I gave her a quick kiss on the cheek, being careful not to brush up against her clean clothes. She had a fresh outfit laid out for me when I got out of the tub.

Mothers! Well, my mother, anyhow!

I ate a sandwich and drank hot chocolate and lazed around the house. If I fell onto something downtown, it wouldn't be on a Sunday afternoon. Night was a more likely time. My father spent the hours reading and dozing. A Hoosier by birth, he was re-reading Booth Tarkington with only occasional interest. My book was *Catch-22*.

A half-hour after supper I was ready.

The rain had slackened even more and the air grown chilly. Who could be sure, it might really snow? That could and had happened in June.

I parked at the Bar Star. It had just a couple of customers, ranch hands that I knew to speak to. I spoke and at

Tad's gesture followed along to the far end of the bar.

"You got my thanks, Jase," Tad said. "I'm going to team up with you and your crew. Gave notice already."

"So the sheriff was telling me. It suits me fine. You'll make out. How about a short beer?"

He drew it and as I took my first sip said softly so as not to be overheard, "Your man was in town last night."

I matched his tone. "Who is that?"

"Seems I heard somewhere you were on the lookout for Becker?"

"He was in town, huh?"

"For a while, anyhow. He got juiced up pretty good. I thought you'd want to know."

"Did he say where he was going?"

"Not to me. He had just got back from trucking some cattle. I guessed he was going back to Chuck Cleaver's ranch, but he didn't say so. He could have passed out." Tad leaned across the bar, closer to me. "You think he's guilty?"

"Mr. Charleston does the thinking. He hasn't told me."

"Well, anyhow, I told you what I know. I feel like a member of your gang already."

"Keep it up, Tad," I said. We shook hands. I finished my beer and went out and sat in the car. After what might pass for thought, I got out and crossed the street to the Commercial Cafe. If there was any official purpose in talking to Jessie Lou, I didn't know what it was. Still, I went.

There were only a couple of late diners inside. One girl, a stranger, was waiting on them. The other was clearing the tables after what looked like pretty fair business. I knew her casually. Jessie Lou wasn't in sight.

The fat fry cook behind the counter was picking his teeth. I walked over and asked, "Where's Jessie Lou?"

"A-ha," he answered, almost losing the toothpick. "Don't blame you. She's some dumpling."

"No cracks," I told him. "Just answer. Where is she?"

"Pardon me all to hell, officer. She called up sick." A note of grievance came into his voice. "We needed her, too. Needed her bad. Had to hire a green gal in her place."

"Did she say what was wrong?"

"You don't ask a young lady that question, now, do you? Sick is what she said and sick, I guess, is what she is."

Back in the car, I sat and wondered. Becker in town: Jessie Lou off work. Connection there? Did the facts jell? There was no harm in finding out.

The curtains were drawn at Jessie Lou's house and no lights shone in the windows. But sick people didn't always want light, and there was enough still in the sky to give the house some. I went to the door and rang the bell, rang it again, then again. The door opened a bare crack. A voice got through the crack. "Jase, I can't see you. I'm not fit to be seen."

I had to push my way in.

Even in the murk of the room I could see swelling on the left side of her face. One eye was so close to shut as to leave only a slit. Before morning it would be blacker, more discolored, than it already was. These things I noticed first. She was dressed in a wrinkled wrapper and wore overrun bedroom slippers. The word that jumped to my mind was woebegone.

"What?" I said. "Just what? What in hell?"

Her voice was frail. "I didn't want to see you this way.

No. Don't turn on the lights. I can't even stand to look at myself."

"Forget that! Let's sit down. Then you can tell me. You'll have to tell me."

She moved back and slumped on the sofa while I took a chair. "I earned it, I guess. The wages of sin as they say."

"Just tell me."

"Oh, damn it, Jase! Damn it! The chickens came home to roost."

"One chicken, you mean? One chicken named Becker?"

She swallowed. I thought that act hurt her. She bent her head and put her hands to her face and spoke almost in a whisper. "He forced his way into my house. He tried to force me to—you know. He hit me. You can see that. But don't look anymore, Jase."

"Why didn't you call me? Call someone? You could have done that."

"Not then, I couldn't. Not later, either. My word? What's it worth? A laugh. Just another fight in a whorehouse."

The words rather than Jessie Lou herself made me mad. "It's not a whorehouse anymore, and for God's sake quit accusing yourself! Stop right now! I know you."

"That's the trouble. You know. A lot of people know or suspect. What's the use, Jase?"

How answer? Like a soul-saver? Like Solomon? Seeing her huddled there in the darkened room, hearing the frail voice, I wanted to cry out a protest. I wanted to swear. I wanted to hold and to comfort her. I did say, "You fought him off. Why? Because you saw purpose in that. What's the use? Don't ask that fool question. You saw a use for yourself better than his use of you."

One hand came away from her face then, and one big eye looked at me. "I did fight him off, Jase. He didn't succeed. He did not. You have to believe me. I got away and ran out the back door."

"I believe you. Did he try to catch you?"

"I'm not sure, but he couldn't catch me, never ever."

"No?"

It might have been my imagination, working there in the gloom, but I thought I saw a crinkle of smile around that one eye. "Never. Bowlegs and cowpuncher boots?"

I felt we were on better footing, so asked, "Do you know where Becker went? Did he say?"

"No. To the ranch, I suppose."

"Not to Breedtown?"

She gave me her full face. Even lopsided, it was pretty. You could tell what she really looked like. She said, "He wouldn't dare."

"Why not?" I asked, though the answer lay plain enough.

"Eagle Charlie."

"If Becker killed him, yes."

"He was hot after Rosa, and Eagle Charlie wouldn't make terms. There's a good reason."

"Maybe so, Jessie Lou, but that motive seems weak to me."

"How many men have been killed over a woman? You're an innocent, Jase."

She was getting some of her spirit back, and I was glad.

I got up, resisting an impulse to take her in my arms. I said, "You're one hell of a girl, Jessie Lou," and went out, knowing she was.

The rain had ceased altogether. In its stead was cold. It would be freezing cold in the mountains. If it didn't rain more and soon, the flood was a flash.

I thought about going to Charleston's apartment to report what I'd learned but voted no. He was up there with Geet, relaxing, enjoying privacy. Tomorrow would be time enough.

I did go to the Jackson Hotel and asked if Dave Becker was registered. He wasn't.

So home for me.

Chapter
Seventeen

THE MORNING was crisp, almost as if touched by frost. Water still ran in the gutters and puddled the low spots, though no more than last night. The whole arch of the sky was clear blue. The sun was only trying to warm up. No flood of great consequence, I told myself.

I walked halfway to the office before I remembered I had come home in the county car—on official business approved by the sheriff. I walked back and got it running.

Inside the office I found Jimmy giggling. It wasn't like him to giggle at any time, much less at ten minutes of eight.

"What's up?" I asked. "Feathers in your britches, Jimmy?"

"You missed yesterday," he said. "You missed the whole show. Your bad luck." Remembrance made him laugh.

"You could tell me."

"I will, seein' as the sheriff hasn't come in." He giggled some more. "God and a pisspot, but it was funny!"

I sat down and waited.

"It was your Mr. Jesus. He showed up lookin' like he'd been drug through a mile of old culvert. Soppin' wet and dirtied up, and he come in with any importance he had left, and his shoes was slickery, and he fell down right there." He pointed to a place on the floor and laughed again. "It didn't hurt him, the fall on his ass, I mean, but it sure put a dent in his dignity. I like to split a gut, tryin' to keep sober-sided just then, but later I let myself go. Talk about a comedown!"

"Tell me the rest," I said. "What went on before?"

"I'm comin' round to it. What happened was he met Luke McGluke out on the road, both of them in cars, and he squeezed Luke off to the side and got out to put questions to him. Luke, he knew his old wreck wouldn't outrun a lame goose, so he popped out of it and took out on foot, across the fields, throwin' mud with each jump, and behind him came Gewald."

Jimmy chuckled as the scene formed in his mind. "You know how damn wet it was. Maybe they run a mile— Gewald allowed it was two—but Luke was too scared to be caught. So Gewald went back to his car and come to the office. That's when he fell on his butt. It did me good, I tell you. Old high-and-mighty sittin' surprised on his behind, wet as a drowned rabbit and muddy to boot. He was one sore-assed inspector, the bruise to his feelin's bein' worse than a broke hip."

I kept grinning. "What next?"

"I gave Gewald time to get his clothes changed and then coaxed Luke into the office. He'd come back by then and was hidin' out in his lean-to. The sheriff took the board while I was gone."

"Keep going."

"I had to sit in on the interview, or Luke would have flown the coop. What came of it? Just what you'd expect. Not a damn thing. Luke, he just looked loco, and his answers were straight, I guess, but dim-like. I felt sorry for him. Gewald didn't. He kept leanin' on him, like he expected sense to come out of a funny farm."

The door opened to admit Charleston. After we'd said hello, he took me to the inner office.

I could hardly wait to sit down. "Becker's back."

He wanted to know where and how I'd picked up that fact, and I told him the whole story.

"So we have at least a case of assault and battery against that no-good," he said.

"I doubt Jessie Lou would testify."

"Maybe not. So you think Becker went back to the Cleaver ranch?"

"That's my guess. Where else? He was ahead of the flood. The bridge hadn't washed out."

Charleston picked up a pencil and turned it in his fingers. "I talked to the foreman of the road crew this morning. They'll put in a temporary bridge, but it won't be passable until tomorrow. One day of grace for Mr. Becker. We'll just sit tight."

"I hear Mr. Gewald had his troubles?" I said.

"You might say so," he answered, grinning. "The bright side is that Jimmy's in fine spirits. All's right with his world."

"Is Gewald coming around today?"

"Later on, I suppose. He's determined to get to Breedtown and bring those two women in. For him I got the loan of a four-wheel drive from the county road shop. That comes under the head of professional courtesy."

I thought the courtesy was overdone but didn't say so. I asked, "Has he started out yet?"

"No idea, Jase."

"What's for me to do?"

He lighted his first cigar of the day. "Stick around. Wait

developments. Relieve Jimmy, maybe, or Halvor tonight. Attend to what calls might come in."

He leaned back and blew smoke at the ceiling as if no matters pressed on him. "Did you ever read any criminal psychology, case histories, psychiatric studies, explanations, that sort of thing?"

I said I hadn't.

"They don't make much sense, if I'm any judge. According to them no one is a criminal. Behind every crime are personal reasons, compulsions, distortions of personality, explanations that to me in most cases are merely excuses."

When Charleston was off and running—an infrequent event—I didn't interrupt.

"A child is treated too strictly, so, grown up, he hates mama or papa or the whole world. He's punished for wetting the bed, so as an adult he wants to pee on the universe. Or he's ordered to use his right hand when he's a natural lefty and so his spirit's deformed. Or he finds mama and papa engaged in the act, and he loves mama himself and so develops a complex. Or, somehow, for reasons that require a lot of expert explanations, he becomes a sex fiend with a set on little girls. All can be explained, and so all is forgiven. Tommyrot."

Charleston had to relight his cigar.

"The worst of it is that nothing is definite. One practitioner says one thing, a second another and a third still another. Put them on the witness stand and they lean toward their fee. Hell, they fall for it. Where the money is, there's the diagnosis."

I dared to say, "You think there's no honest difference of opinion?"

"Difference of guesses, made different by who pays the

fees. The evidence of that is there in the court records. Godalmighty, Jase, if we had that good a case against anyone, we'd have our murderer."

He smiled as if in apology for talking too much. It struck me, not for the first time by far, that he could talk like a well-educated man, which he was, when he wanted to. Then he sobered and went on. "I suppose I oversimplify. I suppose I speak like a single-minded cop. But let it go. Forgive the child, maybe, but accuse the man. That's where I stand. A son of a bitch is a son of a bitch, and no analysis can excuse him."

He took a breath and said, "Now we'll take up the offering."

"Gewald would agree."

"We'll give him that much credit, then." He took a book out of his desk. "Nothing to do but wait for him."

I went out and talked to Jimmy, who was still Merry Sunshine. He didn't want to be relieved but asked if I would bring him a sandwich and some food for his customers. One of them had been caught with a stolen chain saw and couldn't make bond. Amussen had collared him. The other had been drunk and disorderly, so disorderly as not to be dismissed as simply drunk. Amussen's work again.

I loafed around town for a while, for it wasn't time for lunch yet. Then I went to the Commercial Cafe—Jessie Lou wasn't on shift—had a hamburger and coffee myself and went out with the grub Jimmy had asked for.

I delivered the orders and walked in to see Charleston. He was still reading, and I sat down and played dumb. The telephone interrupted our session. Jimmy spoke to me from the board in the other office. He used the tone

of a professional receptionist. "A gentleman and two ladies to see Mr. Charleston."

Gewald had learned some manners.

I reported to Charleston, "Gewald's here with the
women."

"Tell Jimmy to show them into the file room. I'll be
there directly."

He took his time. He looked at his cigar and settled it
on a tray. He stretched. He rose slowly, saying, "Better
bring your pad, Jase."

Gewald had his visitors seated when we entered and
had taken a chair himself. Charleston went over and sat
behind his desk, first nodding to the two women. I found
a place out of the line of fire.

Before I did, however, I took a long look at the old
woman. She had a sack of a dress and had a blanket drawn
over her shoulders. From her headband two braids de-
scended, one cut off short, in respect to the deceased, I
supposed. Her Indian face said, "No comment, damn
you!"

But Rosa! She wore a red dress, drawn in at the waist
with a sash. Her black hair, let fall, made a striking contrast with the red of her outfit. Though of course she
hadn't, she might have dressed for me, for red and black
were my favorite combination. She hadn't mangled her
hair or cut off a finger or otherwise disfigured herself,
unless in places I couldn't see.

Her face stumped me. How describe it except in loose
words like lovely? It looked sensuous, marked by an in-
held vitality. Her skin had the tinge of copper. Her features were regular rather than fine, but they went together in a way to halt a man's breath. It came to me, as

I seated myself, that she proved the benefits of miscegenation. It was hard to think, it hurt to think, that time would make her dumpy and wrinkled.

Gewald looked to Charleston, and Charleston said amiably, "Go ahead. It's your turn."

Gewald wasn't one to circle around. He was a hammer-and-tongs man. He fastened his gaze on Mrs. Gray Wolf and said, "You hated Eagle Charlie, isn't that so?"

No reply. He might as well have addressed granite. Rosa sat impassive, though that word never could quite apply. Some private spirit resided in her, even when she sat without speech or motion.

"Answer me! Did you hate him? Did he hate you?"

Another pause with nothing to mark it. "All right, you two quarreled. Yes or no?"

While he waited for a reply he didn't get, I found myself stacking Rosa up against Jessie Lou. Rosa had a quality Jessie Lou didn't. She had that appearance of surging inner life, of basic and primitive impulse. Yet, in spite of what I knew about her, she gave the impression of purity, strongly mixed with the challenge to violate her. Blend those two elements, and a man wants to assert his virility. It struck me that few things were so seductive as innocence, real or imagined. A man couldn't wait to erase it. Why did I vote for Jessie Lou, then?

After waiting, Gewald said, "Forget it for now. Have you an idea, any idea at all, about the murder of Eagle Charlie? Any notion about who wanted to kill him?"

If she did, it stayed within the dark stone of her.

Abruptly Gewald turned to Rosa. "Doesn't she speak English?"

"No, sir."

"Can't or won't speak it?"

"She won't if she can. You can ask her."

"How in God's name do I ask her? In the unknown tongue?"

Rosa turned half-around to me in appeal. Innocence beleaguered and in need of help. I didn't fall into that trap, if that's what it was. She shrugged at Gewald.

"You ask her then, you Rosa. You can translate what she says. Didn't she have it in for Eagle Charlie?"

Rosa asked, talking Indian, and got the same reply Gewald had. None.

Gewald switched his attack. "All right, Rosa or Mrs. Charlie or whatever they call you, she did hate Eagle Charlie. Right?"

"They argued, that's all."

"About what?"

"He wasn't Indian enough to suit her."

"In what ways?"

The girl spread her hands. They were small. They seemed too delicate for Breedtown. Her moccasined feet were small, too. "Little things," she said. Her hands, spread, accented proud breasts. "She is Indian, all Indian. That's how she wants to be. Eagle Charlie wasn't that way. He was a good friend of white men. He was—how do I say it—one of the boys. They bought him drinks. He bought them drinks. He cut his hair."

"And that's all?"

"My husband was a chief like his father and grandpa. She wanted him to act like the old chiefs. That's all I know and all I will say. We go now."

"No, by God!" Gewald took a wheezy breath. Heat had been building up in him. The lines in his face, not his

complexion, showed that much. He was a man who
wanted to go places and couldn't get started. "You'll stay
right here till I'm through with you. Hear?"

The girl appealed to me again. I tried a smile.

"How did you feel about Eagle Charlie?" Gewald asked
her. "Not good, I bet?"

"He was my husband."

"Some husband he was. Traded you off for a piece of
beef. Traded you to Grimsley, for Christ's sweet sake!
That suited you, did it? It was fine and dandy?"

The girl bowed her head. She looked at me under fine
brows. She was not innocence beleaguered but innocence
betrayed, needing a friend. She answered, "I did what he
said."

"But you didn't like it? Or did you?"

If the old woman had moved, I hadn't noticed. She
seemed immovable except for the dark beads of her eyes.
They slid this way and that. Charleston sat silent. I was
glad for the pauses, my notebook and fingers and I were.

"What do you say? It was all right?"

"I came back to my husband. I didn't kill him. He was
good to me."

Gewald snorted, or came as close to a snort as he ever
would. "Sure he was. Like hell he was. Now tell me, who
were his enemies. Who wanted him dead?"

"I don't know."

"Luke McGluke? Red Fall?"

"Why would they?"

"That's what I'm asking. Who?"

"I don't know."

"Eagle Charlie died right on your doorstep, and you say
you don't know. Nuts. Did you hear anything? Did you see

anything? Anything out of the ordinary? Some little thing, maybe? Some clue? Don't hold back on us, I warn you."

"I was asleep."

"You bet. Everybody was asleep. Eagle Charlie and the man who killed him were awake, though. Yet nobody heard. Nobody suspected."

Rosa shrugged again. "I've said all I know."

"You expect us to believe that? We don't. We'll prove it. You can expect more questions, you and your dummy here. Don't you want us to find the murderer? You are the widow."

"It won't bring my husband back. But, yes. Find the man if you can."

Gewald asked Charleston, "You have any questions?"

Charleston said, "I'm satisfied. Will you be around to-morrow?"

Gewald's face asked a question that Charleston didn't answer. He said, "I can be. Later maybe you'll tell me why. Now the thing is to get these two women home. Beard, how about doing that? The truck's outside."

Charleston gave me a bare nod. For once I was glad to oblige Mr. Gewald.

Chapter
Eighteen

EARLY AS I TURNED OUT that next morning, after a phoned request from Charleston the night before, Mother was in the kitchen before me, busying herself with bacon and waffles. A fresh-squeezed glass of orange juice was at my place on the table.

"Mother," I said, "for goodness' sake, you didn't have to get up at this hour. I can rustle for myself."

She turned away from the frying pan and smiled. "I know you can, Jase, but I do what I like. One of these days—" The fork in her hand made a little going-away gesture as she turned back.

"Don't fret yourself about that," I said. "It looks like I'm a permanent guest."

I ate and then kissed her good-bye.

I was a half-hour ahead of my regular starting time when I entered the office. Charleston was waiting for me. Jimmy was just tidying his cot. He said, "Bunch of damn early birds, and no worm in sight." It was a good-natured comment.

Charleston put on his hat. "We'll take off right away. No excess baggage this way. Gewald will be around later. I asked him to."

He didn't say we were going out to get Becker. I knew

that much without being told. Why he wanted Gewald around for the questioning was another matter. Maybe it was just to show that our office knew its business better than he did.

Charleston buckled on the six-shooter that he seldom carried. He didn't explain, and I didn't ask.

"The temporary bridge is in," he said as we walked out to the Special. "I checked, of course."

I repeated, "Of course," and he turned with a grin, as if to acknowledge it was idle to tell me.

The morning was as fair as ever nature could give. The sky was tall, to the end of sight and beyond. The horizons lay peaceful and distant, drowsing under the early sun. I thought of a statement I had read somewhere: values arise by contrast. So, sure, we needed cold and wind and rain for a full appreciation of days like this one.

The Special ran with low chuckles as if it found the fuel mixture just right. The low hills to our right showed a beginning green. To the west the mountains lifted, blue and white. Not a bad combination, either. More restful than red and black. The road was dry, but the borrow pits held the remembered rain. Two pairs of ducks, returned migrants, swam in a small lake that we passed. They had recalled the gorgeous days, too, and come back to enjoy them.

We crossed the temporary bridge over the ditch. A couple of earth movers stood at the side of the road there, idle and silent until hands made them growl. The bridge was narrow, its approaches rough, but it sufficed. Water lay in the ditch, not running. The head gate must have been closed.

Maybe eight miles farther on, we turned to the right, off

the highway, and for about three more miles churned along a muddied dirt road and pulled up in front of Chuck Cleaver's house.

Cleaver answered our knock and smiled a welcome. Charleston greeted him civilly before asking, "Dave Becker here?"

"He's here but not quite. I got a cow calving late, and she's in trouble, so he's pulling the calf. Won't be long."

"All right," Charleston said.

"I told you he'd come back here, didn't I? I had a damn lock on him like I said. Come on in."

He showed us into a small living room, made smaller by lumpy, overstuffed furniture with purple coverings. Purple wasn't my favorite color. Mrs. Cleaver—I guessed it was Mrs. Cleaver—could be heard moving around in the kitchen out of sight.

"I was thinkin' you could have called me," Cleaver said, "but hell. Something out of whack, like the damn telephone, and I keep forgettin'. You know how it is."

"Do it myself."

"Sit down, you two."

My seat was on a spring that was trying to push through the purple.

"I wouldn't ask, of course," Cleaver said, asking, "but I don't know why you're so hot after Becker? He's a good man. I got no kick on his work."

"We may have missed something." Charleston was being patient. "He may have missed it. We're going over the killings again, bottom to top. People forget. People pass over things that didn't strike them in the first place. They need to be nudged. The second or third or fourth time over, they may recall that little something that gives us a clue."

"Maybe so, but Becker says you've pumped him clear dry."

"You never know."

Cleaver cocked an ear. "I think I hear Becker out in back now. I'll go see. It'll be a minute. He'll have to clean up. Messy business, pullin' a calf is."

After he left us, we waited and listened, hearing men's voices and the clatter of a wash basin. A little later the two came in, Cleaver in the lead. "Cow and calf doing fine," he announced cheerfully.

Becker pushed ahead of him and faced Charleston. "Now what in hell do you want?" He stood bareheaded, indignant on his bowlegs, his face tight with what might have been outrage.

Cleaver said, "Take it easy, Dave."

"Take it easy! I've come clean with these jokers. Told them everything that I know. But here they are again with their goddamn questions. Same old questions, same old answers. Jesus Christ! Buttin' in on my work."

Charleston had risen. He said, "Get your hat."

"No, by God! Shoot your questions, Mr. Sheriff. Here or nowhere."

Cleaver asked, "Why not here, Charleston?"

"Because I'm taking him in."

I saw Becker's hands open and close into fists. I saw his eyes go to Charleston's revolver. It struck me that Charleston carried the gun only for effect. I never had known him to use it.

"Shit!" Becker said in a voice loud enough to be heard in the kitchen. He looked again at the revolver. "Be back, Chuck," he said. "Be back after playtime." He went out the front door, followed by us, and walked around to the back and got his hat from a peg over a wash bench decorated with a basin and one dirty towel.

Charleston asked me to drive and got in the back with Becker. Considerate of him, I thought, or plain careful, but, if I had to, I could handle Becker myself.

Not one word was said all the way back to town. Not a one. The only sounds were the hum of the engine and, once, the squawks of two ducks flushed from their home in the borrow pit.

It was hard to believe, on this quiet and tranquil morning, that murder could have been done, that violence could exist. Had the killer only counted to ten, so to speak, a day like today would have soothed him. The whole sky said peace.

Gewald was waiting when we entered the office. At Charleston's bidding he got up and followed us, not into the file room but this time into the inner office.

We sat ourselves at Charleston's direction, me with my notebook. He settled himself behind his desk. Facing Becker, he asked a peculiar question. "Knock-em-dead?" He paused. "That ring your bells, Becker?"

Becker seemed honestly puzzled. He looked at Gewald, then me, as if to find answers there. At last he said, "Knock-em-dead? What in Christ's name? Sure, I've heard it. Football fans yell it, prizefight fans, too, and hockey fans for all that I know. Make sense, man."

"Never mind," Charleston said, waving the question aside. "It's just that two men were knocked dead." He leaned forward, his eyes hard on Becker. "We've got plenty against you."

"Plenty bullshit."

"We'll start small. A case of assault and battery."

Before he took time to think, Becker answered, "I betcha. I beat men up all the time."

"Did I say a man, Becker?"

I could almost hear the gears turning in Becker's head. He burst out, "That little bitch! That little bitch whore!"

"No, Jase," Charleston said. "Sit back down." To Becker he went on, "You admit to that charge, huh?"

"What of it? It's a little damn thing. Hell, nothing. She was selling it but still turned me down, me with money in hand. That burns any man. So I cuffed her, not much. I'll pay the fine, put up bail, or whatever, and that's the end of it."

Charleston pointed a finger. "That's just the beginning, nothing by comparison. I can tell the whole story, or maybe you'd rather?"

"I love to hear fairy tales."

"You don't have to speak."

"I haven't heard nothin' to speak of."

"You can call a lawyer."

"I know my rights, but them bloodsuckers!"

Charleston took a couple of deep breaths as if to find wind for his story. Gewald sat motionless except for his eyes, his hands clasped in his lap. He would break in on the interview if he thought it went wrong. Becker perched forward in his chair, ready to fight.

"You and Eagle Charlie were in cahoots," Charleston said, his tone quiet but firm. "You were rustling Grimsley's beef."

"Bullshit!"

"You got the cows to Eagle Charlie," Charleston went on, ignoring the interruption. "He got them away. And until the last Grimsley trusted you. He trusted your head count. Then he began his own tally. The two didn't agree."

"So what? Whose count always comes out the same? It was them breeds made off with what few was stole. Grimsley said so himself." Becker clamped his mouth shut, his point made.

"He said so, yes, but that was to keep you from knowing he suspected you, too. He wanted to get the goods on you, and you knew it."

"Next thing," Becker said, "you'll say I killed Grimsley."

"That's what I am saying."

Becker started half up from his chair. "You goddamn fool, you! Killed him, for Christ's sake!"

Charleston went on quietly. "Now Eagle Charlie didn't mind making off with a few cows, but he was kind of a friend of Grimsley. He had a good thing in him. He didn't want Grimsley killed. He was upset and sore about that. He made you uneasy."

"It's this crazy crap that makes me uneasy."

"There was another little matter, Becker. You wanted to bed Rosa. You didn't just want to, you were wild to do that."

"All right, I had my eye on her. I own up I wanted to have her. That's natural. What man wouldn't?"

"That would depend on the man," Charleston said dryly, "but let's go on. You knew Rosa had been farmed out to Grimsley. You tackled Eagle Charlie. But you're a tightwad, Becker. You wouldn't pay what he asked. You had words about that."

"We talked, sure. But twenty dollars a night!"

"So you quarreled. You got hot. Damn him, anyway!"

Becker just replied, "So you say."

We all waited for Charleston to continue. Gewald, still attentive as a hawk, seemed about to say something but restrained himself. I hoped my incomplete notes were enough for a final report.

"Two pretty good motives, Becker," Charleston went on after the pause. "Two very persuasive motives. Fear that Eagle Charlie would talk, pants on fire for the wife he wouldn't sell cheap."

Becker hunched forward, his hard face working. "Good God, you crazy fool! Good God! Now you're saying that I killed Eagle Charlie!"

"That's right."

"That's wrong. I was haulin' cattle for Cleaver when Eagle Charlie was kilt."

"That's your word. We have other witnesses. You stuck around long enough to do in your partner."

"A pack of lies, that's what you're tellin'. A loco imagination you got. Guessin' this and guessin' that and no proof at all."

"Enough," Charleston replied. He fingered papers on his desk like a lawyer in court. "I have records of your account at the bank. They show regular deposits of your paycheck, but that's not all. You made irregular deposits, often in amounts bigger than your pay."

"It's a man's own business where his money comes from," Becker answered. His voice still sounded with bluster, but he appeared suddenly smaller, shrunken somehow, as he slid back in his chair.

"So long as it's legal, Becker. Was this money legally made? Where did it come from?"

Becker's tongue darted over his lips like a snake's. "I

own up to one thing, and you'll build a mountain."

There was inquiry in the tone and words, a sort of hopeful self-serving, as if he hunted for a way out, but all Charleston said was, "Things follow each other."

"All right about Eagle Charlie and me. We stole a few head. Grimsley could damn well afford it. If he was lookin' toward me, I didn't know it."

"Not even a hint, huh?"

Becker licked his lips again. "I wasn't plumb easy at any time. You know how it would be? The idea of gettin' caught?"

"I can imagine. Now about Eagle Charlie, about him and the killing of Grimsley?"

"To tell the truth—"

"It's about time."

"We shied off from each other after Grimsley got bonked. That was plain sensible. We didn't want to be seen together after makin' off with a few of his cows. Understand? Too easy to point a finger at us."

"Did Eagle Charlie suspect you?"

"What of?"

"You know what of. Maybe that's why he wouldn't let you have Rosa?"

"Thinkin' I was the killer, you mean? So he put the price out of sight? How nuts can you get?"

Charleston counted on two fingers. "Item one, you were afraid he would talk. Item two, you were sore at him about Rosa."

A touch of bluster came back to Becker. "Who in hell kills a man over a piece of tail?"

"Lots of men have, including you, for that reason and others. The charge is murder, two murders. We'll get more proof, but the case is good as it stands."

The wind went out of Becker and scratched back in. "You make-believe son of a bitch," he said in his throat.

Charleston and I took him back and locked him in a cell. Gewald still sat in his chair on our return. "A little sketchy," he said to Charleston, "but all right. You got your man."

"We'll fill in the gaps."

"Sure thing." For one of the few times I'd seen him do it, Gewald smiled. "Good work, Sheriff."

"Given the time we had, you would have taken him in yourself."

"I was hot on the same track all right, but congratulations. Well, no use for me any longer." He looked at his watch. The clock on the wall said high noon.

Like good companions we went out and had lunch.

Seated back in the office, with Gewald gone, Charleston informed me, "It has been said that there's more than one way of skinning a cat."

"What cat?"

"Gewald. We got rid of him, didn't we?"

"By beating him to the punch."

Charleston locked his hands behind his head and yawned and for a little while didn't say anything. Then, "It won't hurt him to spend time in jail. It just may help his soul."

"Becker?"

"Who else? We got him to involve Eagle Charlie. I was guessing."

"It was a good guess," I said. "But the rest wasn't guessing. No, sir. You knew."

"Take the charges in some kind of order, Jase, not that they're charges in fact yet. Becker is guilty of assault and battery. Guilty as hell and admitted. But Jessie Lou doesn't want to testify, and I don't blame her. No case, then."

He took his hands from his head and let them lie idle on the desk. "Rustling cattle. Grand larceny. Guilty again and admitted. But Grimsley left no will and has no relatives at all, none that have been found to date. So who's to press charges? With Eagle Charlie out of the picture, where's the evidence? Just the bank records, and they alone aren't conclusive. If the estate were to act through an administrator or executor or anyone else—that's unlikely—but if it happened, even a dumb defense lawyer could win hands down. I said we were lucky to get Eagle Charlie involved. Well, only to confirm a guess. It cuts no ice in the end. So there again, Jase, no case."

I said, not believing, "You sound like you're throwing everything out of the window."

"Oh, I think we make progress, but still you're right. You see, Jase, Becker's not guilty of murder."

Chapter
Nineteen

I WAS UP in decent time the next morning and just
strolled to the office. The events of yesterday and all the
days before swam around in my head. I felt too dull to put
them in order or to reach for conclusions. They were just
changing pictures and scraps of conversation without se-
quence or destination. A tired man made a poor thinker.

I had relieved Halvor the night before and not knocked
off until after the bars closed. I might as well have been
in bed except for one minor incident. I had had to put the
run on three kids who were raising a ruckus at Hamm's
Big Hamburger.

Kids, I thought as I lazed along. Kids were a constant
annoyance, though not a real menace to life and limb if
you ignored their own. Not so, though. Not quite so. Put
a brash and headlong kid—they weren't all that way by far
—put him or leave him at a steering wheel, and God save
all parties. But what to do? Run them in, and they were
put under the supervision of a juvenile-court officer, who
was qualified because his own kids were obstreperous beyond his control. I had to remind myself that I was a kid
once, not too long ago. A few years could make a whole
lot of difference in behavior and attitude.

The door to the inner office was open when I pushed in

at the front, but Charleston was not in his chair. Jimmy sat
at the board.

"Not here yet, huh?" I asked Jimmy.

"Been and gone. On again, off again."

"Where? Did he say?"

"Nobody tells me one damn thing." It was plain that
Jimmy had recovered from his attack of good cheer. "All
I do is answer this fool phone, turn keys and pack grub to
our guests. Yeah, indispensable like they say, that's me."

"Nuts, Jimmy," I said. "No cause to bitch. No one could
do your job as well as you do." A little praise often bucked
him up, but not now.

"Like hell! I'm a discard. You go in there with him and
close the door, you or him, one. I'm too big a risk to be let
in on the know. That's the shape of it."

I sat down. "He closes the door so the phone won't
break in on what he's thinking and doing. He knows you'll
ring him on anything important. That's what you do. Sift
the calls."

"Never knowin' what goes on."

"All right. What do I do? I scribble notes. I don't know
what's up half the time. Let's both go on strike." Jimmy
began to look a little less cranky, and I switched the subject. "How's our new customer?"

"Becker? That bowlegged bastard? I got a mind to
order up a barrel so he'll have a comfortable seat. How is
he? As well as could be expected seein' he's got a hard
dose of lockjaw. Won't say hello or shit or get out, but who
gives a damn? You got him cold, Jase?"

"You'll have to ask the sheriff. I thought we did but
don't know for sure now. Just one thing I do know. I'd like
to give him a good working over."

The clock on the wall had crept along toward nine o'clock. I asked, "When did Charleston take off?"

"Early. I hadn't even rolled out. I'm supposed to tell you to stick around. Almost forgot that."

I went to my desk and began typing up my report. My scatter of notes, plus concentration, brought back the said words.

A half-hour later Charleston brought in Red Fall. "I'm entirely willing to help," Fall was saying, "but why bring me here? You haven't told me, though I keep asking."

"Take a chair," Charleston answered. "Morning, Jase."

Fall nodded to me and sat down at the side of the desk. "I could be working, you know."

"So you've said before. I'm sorry my work interrupts yours." Charleston's reply didn't sound sorry.

I had turned in my chair and moved closer, ready for notes.

Charleston took a cigar from his pocket, rolled it in his fingers, regarded it and decided not to light up. Almost casually, except that his eyes were alert, he asked the question that had puzzled me yesterday.

"Mr. Fall, you have heard of a knock-em-dead?"

There was an instant of silence, a hanging silence that seemed to clang bells. Fall sat, motion suspended.

"I'll show you what I mean." Charleston opened a desk drawer. He pulled a cow's tail—a cow's tail—out of it and laid it on the desk. It was the tail of a red cow. It was lumpy with something that couldn't be bone. I had time to see that much.

A sort of squawk, a kind of shriek, came out of Fall. He snatched the tail up by one end and swung it back, aiming at Charleston.

I dived at Fall. We went down to the clatter of chairs. I heard Charleston's "Hold him!" and felt Charleston's hands reaching beneath me.

It was all scramble and squirm. Fall was wiry and fast as a weasel. He got away from me. He wrenched free from Charleston. He ran for the door with me on his heels and Charleston on mine.

Fall crashed through the inner door and charged toward the outer, and there, crowding the doorway, big as a Percheron, stood Halvor, ignorant but ready for action.

At the sight of him Fall spun around and faced me. His hand with the tail swung back for the strike. A hard swipe from behind knocked me over. I heard the hissing swish of the tail as it tore by my ear. Then my head hit the wall. It struck the baseboard.

I climbed to my feet, using the wall to steady me. When I turned around, Jimmy was putting handcuffs on Fall while Charleston and Halvor held him tight.

"Good enough," Charleston said. "Watch him, though." We were all breathing short. He turned to me. "Sorry I had to knock you out of the way. That thing would have killed you."

"You, too."

"I caught him at the end of the swing. Oh, at the desk. Right. Thanks for the dive, Jase." He straightened his clothes and ran a hand through his hair. "Now, Mr. Fall," he said as if nothing had disturbed his composure, "shall we continue our discussion?"

We steered Fall back to the inner office, leaving the door open. Jimmy would have no kick coming now. He and Halvor edged inside. Fall seemed tame enough. Seated, he said, "You stole it from me." The words were inquiry, not accusation.

"No, I made my own knock-em-dead. We'll find yours at the dude ranch." Charleston settled himself in his chair. "A few questions now. Better answer them."

As if in prayer, Fall's head was bent over his cuffed hands.

"You killed Grimsley and Eagle Charlie." The words weren't put as a question.

" 'Vengeance is mine saith the Lord.' "

"So it is written. What sayest thou?"

I sneaked a glance at Jimmy and Halvor, standing at the door. Their faces showed the astonishment I felt. Charleston couldn't be ridiculing the man. More likely he was pretending to join the evangelical league in order to lead him on.

There wasn't much time to speculate, for Fall came on with "They were abominations in the sight of God."

"Verily."

"They trafficked in her flesh. They were forcing her soul to hell, her immortal soul."

"The soul of Rosa?"

"The soul of Rosa. 'The Lord knoweth the way of the righteous, but the way of the wicked shall perish.' "

Now matter of fact, Charleston said, "So you took it on yourself to remove them?"

Fall's head jerked up. I hitched around so as to have a better view of his face. The one eye I could see had the straight glare of fanaticism in it. "Not on myself. Not for myself. It was ordered."

"I see. Who issued the orders?"

"You do not see. You cannot see. It was the Lord's will."

Charleston said as an aside, "It's a little difficult to jail God."

The mad stare held steady. Fall spoke as if Charleston

hadn't. "I was His agent. He spoke to me. I heard His voice."

Charleston's head moved from side to side, slowly, as if heavy with understanding. "So you played God."

"That's evil. That's blasphemous. He gave the word. I was His humble servant."

Fall put his cuffed hands to his face. After a moment I knew he was crying. Mutters came from him, I supposed words of supplication.

Charleston gave him time for his prayers. Then he said mildly, "How did you know about Rosa?"

"From the old Christian lady. From Mrs. Gray Wolf. She hated sin. Then I watched to make sure." Fall lifted his wet face. He seemed comforted and resigned.

"The assignment must have been difficult."

"Not with God's help. I had time. I studied their habits, their movements."

"You refer to Eagle Charlie and Grimsley?"

"They were both older men. They had to get up at night. The toilets are on the outside."

"All for Rosa," Charleston said. He paused and asked, "How do you feel about Rosa?"

Fall's cuffed hands moved small in their prison. "She is God's work."

"So are we all, but you haven't answered my question."

"There is no shame in it." Together the hands moved up and down. "You want to make it shameful."

"Not unless it is. Go on."

"I love her, love her as you can't understand."

"I presume you have had her? I gather you wanted to save her for yourself alone."

Fall tried to gesture. The cuffs restrained him. Jimmy

and Halvor stood silent, too intent to whisper or move. The phone rang, but they didn't stir. Fall said, "I knew you would see shame in pure feeling. Only the carnal has a place in your interest."

"It has some place all right."

"The one place. The only place. When I say I love her, you make it animal love, that alone. May the Lord help you. May He lead you to understanding."

Charleston sounded tired when he spoke. "So, since you loved her, God asked you to remove her defilers."

He shook his head again and rose. "I'm sorry, Mr. Fall, but in our society the laws of man come first. Under them we have to lock you up."

"May God have mercy on you."

We locked him up.

Chapter
Twenty

LATE THAT AFTERNOON I returned to the office, where I found Charleston waiting. He had sent me home after Fall was put in a cell, saying, "Go on, Jase. Take some aspirin, have a nap. You look done in. A few more knocks on that skull of yours, and I'll have to call you knot-head." He added, "Then maybe you'll feel well enough to come out to our place and have dinner with Geet and me."

I wasn't much in favor of rest and a nap, but my head did pound, each pulse of blood being a reminder of hurt, and I was draggy, what with too little sleep and the wear and tear of the day. I fell asleep on the couch at home while trying to figure out how Charleston had come to fasten on Fall. Twice, drowsing, I heard Mother tiptoe into the room. Nothing to wonder about there. She wanted to make sure I was warm enough and all right.

Charleston sat alone in the office when I arrived. Jimmy, I supposed, had gone out to eat. "Feeling better?" Charleston asked after sizing me up.

"As good as new, if that's saying anything."

He seemed satisfied with my appearance. "I've been putting off what has to be done. Let him think on his sins, I've been telling myself. But the sad time has arrived. Come along."

He rose and took the jail keys from their hook, and I

followed him back to the cells. He unlocked the one that held Becker. Becker was sitting on his bunk. He didn't get up. "More damn foolishness?" he asked, his eyes squinting.

I caught a glimpse of Red Fall in the cell adjoining. He was lying down, his eyes open, praying or meditating, I guessed. Whatever it was, it shut us off from any open attention.

"Get out, Becker," Charleston said. "You're free for now."

It took a second for the words to leak through. Then Becker got up. "I told you. I been tellin' you—"

"I remember. Now it's my turn to tell you. Get just one little bit out of line again, do one little thing, and you'll wish to God you hadn't. Hear that?"

"Don't worry." Becker thumbed toward Fall's cell. "I'm converted. I heard enough prayers to save the whole goddamned world."

Fall's spoken words followed us out. "May God go with you. Believe in the Lord."

Becker moved ahead of us, making for the outer door, his boots canted to the slant of his legs.

"You sure kept me in the dark," I told Charleston when we were seated again. I thought, too late, that I sounded peevish, as Jimmy had earlier.

"Sorry, Jase," Charleston replied easily. He finally lit the cigar he had forgotten on his desk. After it was going, he went on, "A man has a crazy idea, a wild hunch, and, if he looks ahead, he keeps it to himself. What if it doesn't pan out? He'll be up a tree. He'll be up the creek, and no paddle. Respect? I want to save whatever I have, and that includes yours, Jase."

"You'd have mine, regardless."

"Don't be too quick to say that." He smiled at me through the smoke. "What if a little vanity comes into the picture? I admit to my share of it. What if I wanted, even a little bit, to collar the murderer all by myself? There's something there, Jase."

"It doesn't change my opinion." In the face of his honesty I was uncomfortable, and it was my fault for having let out a peevish squawk. He didn't have to explain. "You caught Fall, and that's it, and no one else could have done it."

"With the help of others, I caught him. Remember that help. We caught him, Jase. We. So I can't be too proud of myself alone."

"All right, Mr. Charleston, but I still don't savvy. I mean the whole thing. What led to one thing and what thing to another."

He had to relight his cigar. "I was about to explain when you sidetracked me."

He squirmed in his chair for greater comfort and leaned back. "The clue was there from the first. Doc Yak and Felix missed it, or anyhow missed its importance. Jase, Grimsley's skull was broken not just in one place. It was dented and broken through here and there. No pattern to those fractures. Random, you might call them, but curved with the slope of the bone. You remember they talked of a blunt instrument and then a blackjack, but neither one fit the bill. You can see why. A blunt instrument doesn't bend, and a blackjack loaded with shot wouldn't leave those uneven marks. Then came Eagle Charlie. Same thing with him."

Charleston bent forward to put his cigar on a tray and resettled himself. "What was the weapon, then? What could be the genuine article? I set myself to find out."

"Those red hairs, too," I said. "You had to account for them?"

He nodded. "Part of the genuine article. Seems simple now, doesn't it?"

"It had me stumped."

"Me, too, at the time."

"What put you onto it? What brought it to mind?"

He didn't answer the question just then. "We know the locals pretty well, Jase. None seemed to me right for the murders or right for the weapon. But two men we didn't know much about—Becker and Red Fall. Both hail from the Southwest. So I went to the books."

He grinned in remembrance. "You can call me an authority now, a bookworm authority. Ask me about the Graham-Tewksbury feud, and I'll tell you. Ask about the Lincoln County War, and I'll give you the dope. The Gadsden Purchase? Sure, I know all about that. Fringe benefits, that reading was. Not to the point."

He picked up the cigar again, put a match to it and blew a remembering puff. "Then I lucked into Slim Ellison's book, *Cowboys Under the Mogollon Rim.* And there it was, the knock-em-dead. It was known to the Indians of the Southwest, sometimes used by them, I suppose. With that reference I had what I needed."

He came forward and opened a drawer and drew out the cow's tail. "Look at this thing. See the length of it. What a swipe you could give! Knock down a buffalo bull."

I leaned forward to see better.

"I stuffed it with rocks, Jase, just plain old rocks, as the Indians did. What you do, you stitch them in with rawhide or something tough, then sew up the end. Maybe those

Indians got the bone out without cutting the hide on the tail and stuffed it from the root end. I don't know, and it doesn't matter. There it is. Red hairs, too."

"I would have thought first about Becker. I guess you did, too?"

"I didn't count him out, he's so damn ornery. But, when I mentioned it to him, it seemed pretty plain he didn't know about knock-em-deads. What's more, his motives appeared pretty weak, much as I blew them up. One more thing: Rosa and Eagle Charlie aside, he wasn't pally with Indians. He didn't give a hoot about them or their ways or their history. Not Mr. Becker. That left Red Fall!"

"And they'll prove him insane."

"Yep. No doubt about that. And after a while they'll send him from the asylum, saying he's been rendered harmless." Charleston shook his head. "It makes a man wonder."

He shrugged off his wonderment. Gloom never rode him for long. "We're left with a tag end, Jase. We better talk about it." He stubbed out the cigar. His eyes held a question.

I said, "All right."

"There's the little matter of the reward? The little matter of one thousand dollars?"

"You solved the case. It's yours by right."

"Nice going, Jase." The corners of his mouth turned up in a half-smile. "The judge rewards the judge. That funny business aside, I wouldn't take the money."

"But you're entitled to it."

"I said forget it. But don't you forget I had help. There's you, for instance."

"I was just ramming around, getting nowhere. I

wouldn't accept the reward, either. You say forget it, and I say forget it."

"So we'll just let it go unclaimed?"

An idea hit me, and before I had time to examine it, I broke out, "Jessie Lou."

"I was hoping you would say that, Jase."

"But—but she put us on a false trail."

"Not so false. Call it parallel, a parallel trail that finally more or less slanted into the true one. Without knowing about Rosa, thanks to Jessie Lou, where would we have been?"

"You mean—you really mean—Jessie Lou."

"Good boy, Jase. Sure I mean."

"Can I tell her?"

"Who else?"

"Right now?"

Charleston was smiling, smiling his big smile. "I don't see any leg irons on you. Meet me at the Bar Star afterwards. I do think we deserve a drink."

On the way to the Commercial Cafe, I think I met Jimmy, carrying grub back to the jail. If I did, I don't remember too well. Presumably I spoke to him.

Jessie Lou was busy. The counter was occupied, and every table. She and another waitress were hurrying around, taking orders, carrying trays. I got her aside just the same. She looked tired and hot and a little put out that I was keeping her from her work. I held her by the arm. Let the customers wait.

"We got him," I told her.

She seemed too distracted to understand.

"The murderer, I mean. It's Red Fall."

"Him? Thanks, Jase. I have to go now."

"No, you don't. You have to stay. There's the reward. One thousand bucks."

"I hope it's yours, Jase. Now excuse me."

"Just a minute, Jessie Lou. Just a minute. Guess what? The sheriff and I talked it over. The reward goes to you."

"Quit kidding. I didn't do anything."

"I'm not kidding. It's yours, all yours."

Her tired face opened, her eyes wide with beginning-to-believe disbelief. At the end of a gasp she said, "Mine?" in a small voice.

"All yours. That's been decided. It's official."

Before all those customers she threw her arms around me and kissed me. I didn't care much. Then she bent her head to my chest. "Oh, Jase!" she said into my shirt. Her back made little trembles under my hand. "Oh, Jase! Now I can get away. Now I can do it."

She drew her face back. Her mouth was broken, and tears shone on her cheeks.

I was damn near crying myself.